A SIMPLY SENSATIONAL SHOW!

TOO MUCH AT STAKE

Also written by Pat Ondarko & Deb Lewis

Bad to the Last Drop

TOO MUCH AT STAKE

PAT ONDARKO &
DEB LEWIS

LANGDON STREET PRESS
MINNEAPOLIS

Langdon Street Press
212 3rd Avenue North, Suite 290
Minneapolis, MN 55401
612.455.2293
www.langdonstreetpress.com

Grateful acknowledgment is made for permission to use the following materials:
Ballyhoo lyrics by Warren P. Nelson; *Wenabojoo* story by Gerald DePerry;
Farewell Friend lyrics by Pat A. Ondarko; *About Big Top Chautauqua: A History* by
Lake Superior Big Top Chautauqua; Back cover author photo by Carol Seago

ISBN - 978-1-936183-58-6
ISBN - 1-936183-58-7
LCCN - 2010929637

Book sales for North America and international:
Itasca Books, 3501 Highway 100 South, Suite 220
Minneapolis, MN 55416
Phone: 952.345.4488 (toll free 1.800.901.3480)
Fax: 952.920.0541; email to orders@itascabooks.com

Cover Design & typeset by Kristeen Wegner.

Printed in the United States of America

Dedicated to the founders, musicians,

staff, board members, sponsors, volunteers,

and patrons of Lake Superior Big Top Chautauqua,

who have kept the magic of the Tent

alive for twenty-five years

TO YOU, OUR READER, GREETINGS!

We are pleased to bring you, in this, our second mystery, to the site of one of our favorite places on earth.

Lake Superior Big Top Chautauqua (sha-*ta*-qwa) is a non-profit performing arts organization, operating a 900-seat, all-canvas, state-of-the-art tent theater. It is nestled at the base of Mt. Ashwabay (an acronym for the surrounding towns of Ashland, Washburn, and Bayfield) Ski Hill, located three miles south of Bayfield, Wisconsin, overlooking Lake Superior and the Apostle Island National Lakeshore.

We are the real-life counterparts to the main characters, although they are enhanced and embellished in ways that we sometimes wish we were.

We are modern women of a certain age who sometimes are befuddled by cell phones, texting, and Twittering, let alone all the highfalutin gadgets that real investigators seem to have at their fingertips. What we lack in technical know-how, though, we make up for with heart, intuition, and tenacious curiosity. Some might call it stubbornness!

We try to stay away from current politics or cultural events in our mysteries, but sometimes they just seep through our pens onto the page. Aside from the Big Top, many real places are mentioned in this story. We frequent them and want you to know about them in case you decide to pay a visit to the area.

There are great coffee shops in the area. We highly recommend the Black Cat in Ashland, and North Coast Coffee and Chequamegon Book and Coffee Company in Washburn. Patsy's Bar in Washburn has the best hamburgers anywhere. Best chocolates can be gotten at Heike's Blumen Garden and Gabriela's German Cookies and Chocolates in Ashland or Sweet Sailing in Bayfield. Our favorite restaurants are Good Tyme in Washburn and Second Street Bistro in Ashland.

Why did we choose to write about the Big Top? Because of our affection for the people who make it work and our gratitude for the many summer nights of musical magic spent on the ski hill.

As for the truth of the mystery (or any of our other little tales), as our favorite elder, Jessie, would say, "If you tell the story well enough, from your heart, it ends up truth, whether you made it up or not."

We hope you will enjoy reading about our two characters and the adventures that come their way, as much as we enjoyed writing them.

PAT & DEB

PROLOGUE

Who will it be? It seems like forever, this waiting; like being stuck out on the big lake with no wind in your sails. I'll bet I've aged ten years, it's just not fair! It wasn't my fault, if only ... But no use going over it again.

Dusting off the dry mud from his pants and taking out his handkerchief to mop his face, he put his work glove in his back pocket and looked out at the grounds. In spite of the rain, the volunteer crowd numbered about seventy-five. Like a big sleeping giant, the tent's skeleton was put in place, and the sound of the metal against metal was like the waking groans of a mystical being. Alive, that's what it was, and dear god, how he loved it. Restless as he waited, he nervously picked at a spot on his face, playing the game in his mind for the hundredth time. *Who will be the one? Not the very early crew, taking out the big bones with the tractor.* He had known it wouldn't be them.

Earlier, he'd told Phil that he'd strained his back and wouldn't be helping with the heavy stuff today. *Anything so I don't have to go in there.*

Phil had given him a quizzical look and snickered, "More like strained your elbow from lifting a few too many last night, seems to me."

And it was true. He had been drinking heavier lately. "Who wouldn't be?" He didn't realize he had said the words out loud until a volunteer tossed him a questioning glance. He forced a smile and waved him on. His mind and heart raced as if he were running in the Whistle-Stop Marathon in nearby Ashland.

Why didn't I move it? He couldn't even think of it as "him"; it was an "it." *Move it before the winter. But the snow came so early this year, and the skiers were here as soon as the first flakes fell. Damn it!* Truth be told, he couldn't make himself go into that barn again—not with "it" there—let alone drag it to the car. *Anyway, it's way in the back. It would mean getting around all the piles of stuff and dragging that dead weight.* He shuddered but not from the rain that was falling. *I should have tried anyway.* He paced restlessly in front of the chalet but was unable to even look in the barn's direction.

"This is killing me," he muttered, and then the irony of what he had just said made him laugh nervously. "I'll go crazy—no, calm yourself down," he told himself. "You've had six months to prepare for this day. You can do it."

Squaring his shoulders, he turned and quickly walked into the chalet, almost knocking over Deb as she emerged with a cup of coffee.

"Huh, sorry, Deb." He tried to smile, but his thoughts were screaming, *Who will it be? Who will it be?* Absentmindedly, he picked at the scab on his face again. *Think about the great new season we're going to have; think about something else.* But in the back of his mind, the question still rose like a bobber to the surface. *Who will it be? Who will find the body first?*

Deb watched him go, her gaze puzzled; then she shrugged and went back to help the others.

Chapter One

Stinging rain drove into Pat's backside, and icy fingers dripped water down between her Two Harbors yellow rain hat and the collar of her husband, Mitch's, favorite rain jacket, which she had once again conveniently confiscated. *It isn't my fault*, she thought self-righteously, *that he picks out jackets that are so much better than mine. Besides, if he wanted to wear it, he should have gotten up a little earlier.* Closing her eyes to help concentrate, she shivered and dragged the aluminum pole forward another few feet on the slick, muddy grass in front of her. "I will not fall," she chanted under her breath. "I will not fall." *But if I do*, she thought, *that's it. It's into the chalet for me. Let the men put up the darn thing. I don't care if it's sexist or not.* Her feet made squishing noises inside her tennis shoes each time she stepped. It seemed to her as if the tent itself was reluctant to leave the comfort of the large old barn where it had been kept all winter long.

    I don't blame the poor old tent, Pat thought, feeling

cross as she squished along. *If it weren't for opening Friday night …* She sighed, picking up the pipe once more and moving it forward. *But the show must go on. Get over it, Pat. Turn the page,* she chided herself. She looked up just then and smiled at the twinkling brown eyes and elfish face of Sam West, the official photographer for Big Top Chautauqua, just as he snapped a candid shot of her.

It was a normal spring Sunday in northern Wisconsin. "Normal" by Wisconsin standards meant sixty degrees and sunny one day, and a return of winter-like winds the next. Dropping the pole at the feet of one of the men, Pat Kerry saw a face she recognized.

"Is this the one you need, Gary?" she asked hopefully. Pat and her best friend, Deb Linberg, were well acquainted with Detective Gary LeSeur, the handsome male volunteer working beside them today, because he was a police detective from the nearby city of Ashland, where they both lived. Much to Gary's dismay, the women had become entangled with him in an Ashland murder investigation the previous year.

"Hi, Pat," he responded, offering her the wide, slow grin she remembered from their work together—although to be honest, they hadn't *really* worked together on that case. It had been more like "Get out of my hair, you two, before I throw you in jail for obstructing justice." It had all worked out okay in the end, though, and they had even become friends; hence, the smile.

"Sure, that's the right one, but if this rain keeps up, you'd better start bringing out some wooden boards."

Pat looked puzzled. "Boards? I didn't see any boards in the barn. Why do you need them?"

"What else?" he said, rolling his eyes. "To build an ark, of course."

Laughing, Pat went back for another pole. *So many*

people seem to like to make church jokes at me, she thought with a smile, *just because I'm a pastor.*

When Pat had first decided to take a sabbatical from the ministry, she hadn't wanted anyone to know she was a pastor. She had even toyed with the idea of saying that she was a house painter. Pat's smile broadened as she remembered the practical words of her husband, Mitch: "You're such a sloppy painter, Pat. What would you do if someone actually asked you to do a job?" In the end, she decided just not to say anything at all. Now, a year later, she didn't much care who knew. After all, being a pastor was a part of who she was. *Let them deal with it however they want,* she thought. Unfortunately, some folks' way of "dealing with it" was to make church jokes and references.

Oh, well, she thought. She trudged back up the muddy ribbon of grass, ducking her head down as yet another wave of wind hit her straight in her face. *At least when they know, they don't swear so much in front of me.*

Pat's mental reverie was interrupted by the sight of a smartly dressed woman with short, carefully coiffed white hair. Her long azure-blue skirt swished as she walked, and the several gold bracelets she wore on each wrist jangled as she pointed with one hand and clutched a clipboard with the other. Her sweet, grandmotherly voice seemed to coo as she spoke. "This Chautauqua was founded in 1985 by a ragtag bunch of talented musicians, led by one Warren Nelson," she informed the pack of photographers and reporters—all holding notepads and pencils—that she was leading through the construction site. "The 'Big Top,' or 'the Tent,' as it is known to locals, has become a unique, regionally acclaimed performing arts venue, with an annual operating budget of over one million dollars. Making this venue available each summer requires the dedicated efforts of crew and volunteers—they raise it each spring, just before Memorial Day, and take it down each fall, during the week after Labor Day."

Pat looked up at Carolyn Sneed, the long-standing executive director of the Big Top, as she and her entourage approached. "Hello, Carolyn. I guess it's that time once again." Pat nodded amiably at the group.

"Hi, Pat and Deb. Thanks for helping us out this year," Carolyn responded cheerfully.

How does she remember everyone's name? Pat wondered.

Without missing a beat, Carolyn turned her attention back to the news crew. "The process of raising the Tent is done in the spirit of old Chautauquas, or traveling shows, made famous in small towns at the turn of the twentieth century, only this production is done without the elephants to do the grunt work." A few chuckles erupted from the group. "Today, it is the volunteers like Deb and Pat who are the elephants." Carolyn gestured towards them with an impish smile.

"Do I really look like an elephant after all the work I have done losing weight?" Pat whispered under her breath. The group moved on.

Over the past two hours, since Pat was drafted from the food crew into the tent-raising business, she had learned a lot about setting up the tent, and her respect for the dedication of those who worked with the Chautauqua tent show rose considerably. She had been handed work gloves, given a crash course on building a show tent, and sternly advised not to get in the way of the tractor or the machines putting up the huge center poles. In an ideal world, Pat decided, bringing the tuna hot dish and fresh rolls from the Ashland Baking Company Bakery, and helping inside would have been enough.

"Hi, Pat," a voice called from the chalet. "Haven't seen you lately in the Black Cat."

"Hello, Honore. Sure was nice of you to bring out all those muffins," Pat responded. "Would it be too selfish of me to hope you brought coffee, too?" Pat and Honore had become friends the year before when Joe Abramov, a regular at the coffee house was murdered.

"Couldn't have the tent-raising without good coffee," Honore agreed. "I don't guarantee that it won't be gone before lunch, though. Are you working outside this year?"

Pat nodded, shivering slightly. "Yes, but surprisingly, I'm actually enjoying the work."

Well, I'll try to save you a cup for morning break. How's that?" Smiling, Honore went inside the chalet.

Pat certainly wouldn't have enjoyed exercise a year earlier, when she had arrived in Ashland. She had been tired, overweight, and out of shape. But for the last six months, she and Deb had joined Curves, their local gym. *Darned if it hasn't helped*, Pat reflected. Although truth be known, Pat still wasn't above stealing a bite from a great cookie or two.

"Holy crap! Look out!" came an exasperated shout.

Pat looked up the hill to see a pipe rolling down toward her. She jumped out of the way just in time.

"Sorry!" Deb yelled sheepishly, sliding in her wet boots as she ran to stop the pipe—and landed on her rear end in the mud. "Here! Help me up, and let's get this one to the guys. It's the last one," she said, laughing at herself and reaching out a hand to her friend.

Pat felt the little muscles in the small of her back tighten as she bent down to pick up the pipe, but she braced herself, knees bent, and reached out. All the working out had helped build up her muscles around her joints. *Not bad*, Pat thought. *Still, that big 6-0 is coming up. I need to be careful.* She never wanted to be in the position again of not being able to climb a set of stairs.

What the—? Pat thought, as she and Deb both fell down together laughing. They stood up and tried to wipe themselves off with their work gloves.

"Isn't this fun?" Deb called from her end of the pipe. "Next, we get out the rest of the canvases, and a new magical world appears. Aren't you glad you came?" Her bubbly good nature couldn't be kept down by inclement weather and a roll in the mud.

So much for slipping into the nice warm chalet for a cup of coffee, Pat thought, smiling at her friend and seeing the excitement in Deb's eyes. *Besides, those great muffins Honore brought might be all gone by the time we take a break.*

"Need some help over here!" came a call. Laying down the last pipe, the women watched as up and down the hill, a dozen or so volunteers trudged toward the barn to load canvases. When the work was finished, they would be the largest summer tent show in the United States. The canvases were stacked on a large flatbed pulled by an old John Deere tractor.

"What's holding up those canvases?" bellowed a young man in his twenties. His shout startled Deb, causing her to slip once more. "Oops, sorry, Deb!" he said, reaching out a large, firm hand to stop Deb's fall. He had a chiseled face and a lean, strong body that only the young can have. He pushed back his cowboy hat securely on his head, revealing red hair. "Didn't mean to scare you, but it looks like you've made friends with the mud already. Phil Anich is getting ornerier than a she-bear in spring down there." His voice had just a little eastern Canadian lilt. "I s'pose he feels hyper-responsible just because he's the operations manager. And now there's extra pressure—the wind and rainy weather didn't allow us to do this yesterday."

Pat looked curiously at the handsome young man. His hat was a Stinson, she noted, and it had a plastic rain stretcher over it to keep it dry. *That's the only thing that's dry on him*, she thought wryly as she looked at his muddy jeans and cowboy boots.

Deb nudged Pat who, lost in thought, almost fell in the mud again.

"Hey, watch what you're doing, will ya?" Pat reacted.

"That handsome lad you're staring at is Forrest Johnson," Deb whispered. "He's the best homegrown talent that the ski hill and surrounding North Woods has produced in years. Rumor has it that he wants to be a singer like his dad. The talent seems to ooze out of his ears. He can do it all: sing, dance, play the piano, or strum banjo, guitar, or mandolin—everything, that is, except for the fiddle."

Pat turned toward Deb and raised an eyebrow. "Why not the fiddle? Isn't it in his blood?"

Deb nodded her head knowingly. "Funny thing about the fiddle. His mother, Linda, signed him up early for fiddle lessons at the local music school, but Forrest railed against it from the beginning. He stubbornly refused to submit to the strenuous practice schedule—that's a requirement for the young Suzuki students—and insisted he wanted to play the guitar. His mother was so disappointed."

"Like father, *not* like son, you mean?" Pat countered as she moved another batch of stakes. "Why don't our kids ever do what we want, anyway?"

"The eternal question," Deb agreed. "Forrest grew up in the shadow of the Big Top, living in the A-frame at the base of the ski hill on Mount Ashwabay. Their home is just a few hundred yards from the backstage flap on the Tent and a stone's throw from the storage barns where all the show equipment is stored each fall during the second week of September. Didn't I tell you she manages the grounds and property? Quite a woman."

"There seem to be a lot of independent women in these parts," Pat said.

"She's been the caretaker of the ski hill grounds for twenty-three years." Deb smiled pensively. "During the long winters, when the only neighbors are deer, fox, raccoons, porcupines, and rabbits, her cozy home stands sentry in the woods."

"Must be lonely out here when the Tent is done for the season," Pat said.

"Not really," Deb continued, as she dragged more stakes to the next spot designated for a pole. "The ski hill is small but pretty busy. Forrest is a darn good skier, too. Never really got into competition, though. Guess he was too busy helping his mom—it was just the two of them, you know. Still, Linda made sure that her son benefited from the best things that a boyhood in the northern Wisconsin woods offers: affinity with nature and isolation from big-city pressures. That was her thought when she made the difficult decision to keep her child and raise him, single-handedly, in the woods, rather than move to Kansas City to live near her family." Deb sighed. "Forrest has other ideas, though. Kids grow up, and they want to spread their wings."

Pat wasn't listening but was busy with the task at hand. "Deb, how many of these stakes go in each spot again?" Pat brushed away the water that was dripping down her hat into her face.

"Four at each."

"Hey, ladies, we need stakes over here, now!" someone shouted from the other side of the massive tent-in-progress morphing before their eyes.

"When did we become ladies?" grumbled Pat as she picked up more iron stakes and took them to the men who were struggling with the wind and canvas. *When we were young, "ladies" always had "old" in front of it. Is that what I am?* "Boy, if it gets any windier, you guys are going to lift off."

"If it gets any windier, we'll stop for the day. Too dangerous," Phil Anich replied.

Pat wondered if it would be a sin if she prayed for a bit more wind, just so they could stop. *No,* she decided, *not a good idea. Besides, when were my prayers so powerful anyway?* She turned back to Deb, as if they hadn't been interrupted. "So does Forrest get to see his dad much?"

"Some. He only saw his father every couple years when he was growing up—once a year if he was lucky," Deb responded. "Of course, when Monty's group made its annual pilgrimage to perform their fiddling magic on the Big Top stage, he always scheduled a visit for a few weeks with Forrest at the same time. Forrest grew up not knowing that real dads did anything different. Still, the house show band members took him under their wings and shepherded him into manhood and into the musical world. One big happy family. But like I said, Forrest is like a young eaglet ready to take flight. And his dad, Mac … well, Mac is Mac."

"What? Are you saying his dad is Mac? Monty McIntyre from Monty and the Canadian Fiddlers?" The two women sighed at exactly the same time—they were two moms whose children had already left home. *Is any group ever "one big happy family"?* Pat wondered. *For that matter, was there ever a family that was? There's probably more to this story than I will ever know.*

Chapter Two

"Keep it moving, ladies," Forrest said as he walked alongside Deb and Pat. He good-naturedly nudged Deb with his elbow. "We've got to get this tent up today."

"Rain's holding us up. Phil knows that," Deb reassured him. "He's in charge and he's eager for the new season to begin."

"I am, too," the young man admitted. "Ed's going to let me sing with the house band."

"The Blue Canvas Orchestra?" Deb asked.

"Yup. The one and only. Ed and Cheryl sure have added some punch to that band in the last few years," Forrest replied enthusiastically. "It doesn't hurt that he's my godfather."

"Well, then, let's get this big gorgeous blue lady up, because we can't wait to hear that," Pat said, patting him on the shoulder. They came to the large doors on the barn just as the largest canvas tent rolls were put on the trailer.

"Looks like they have enough help with that one,"

Pat said, pulling at her friend's arm to urge her farther into the dry old storage barn. *I've had enough rain and mud,* Pat thought. "Let's see if we can pull some of these smaller rolls closer to the door for them."

"Okay. We can wait here until Phil tells us which roll to take next."

"Good idea," Pat agreed. "By the way, have you seen Mitch and Marc yet? Those dirty dogs were supposed to be here an hour ago." *I wonder if Mitch is looking for his jacket,* Pat thought idly.

"Oh, they're here, all right," Deb assured her. "Marc was helping to tie knots, and Mitch was helping to move the bleachers in place. He'll be sore tomorrow." They laughed together at their middle-aged husbands as only old friends could.

"Hey, ladies!" boomed a deep tenor voice. "Where are your old men?" It was Sam West, holding his camera. "I want to get their pictures!"

Looking over their shoulders down the hill, the women spotted Marc and Mitch in the distance. Deb pointed down at them. "There they are, coming up the hill."

"Thanks," Sam replied as he hurried down the hill to meet them, his camera held aloft.

"How does Marc keep in such good shape?" Pat asked. "He's not having any trouble climbing the hill."

"Oh, you know Marc," Deb replied. "It's all that racquetball and sailing he does when he's not being a doctor. What about Mitch?"

"Mitch gets his exercise on the golf course," Pat said, "and of course in the Midwest, that's a short season." *He will indeed be sore tomorrow, and even the next day*, Pat thought ruefully. *But so will I, I imagine.*

"Girls, need some help over here!" Phil Anich called to them.

"Yes, sir, Mr. Operations Manager, sir!" Pat called back.

They walked cautiously to the far corner of the building—it was dark and musty, as there were only a few hanging light bulbs, and no sunlight came through the windows or the skylight. Pat squinted her eyes in the dim light. A shiver went down her spine, and she felt a rush of discomfort—a queasy feeling in her stomach and a chill in her chest—as she walked farther into the barn. Although it was late May, the room felt cold. *It has an odd, earthy smell*, Pat thought, *like mulch piles after winter, or—*

"Sorry, I meant *ladies*," Phil corrected himself. "I thought the three of us could move this one next." He pointed to a smaller rolled-up canvas. "It shouldn't be a problem, now that the two of you have been getting so trim and strong," he teased. "Take a corner, will you?" Together, the three of them attempted to lift the canvas.

"Oof!" Phil grunted. "That's heavier than I thought." He saw LeSeur coming in the door and called out to him. "Can you lend a hand?"

"Sure," LeSeur said amiably. "Anything to move this along. The rain has stopped, thank goodness, but with a smaller crew we'll be here 'til midnight, not to mention that the band is getting cranky as all get out at the delays." He wiped his wet face with a large handkerchief.

"Well, come on over here then. Quit jawing and lift that corner," Phil directed. "Man, this is so heavy you'd think there was a dead body in it."

As if on cue, the end that Pat and Deb were trying to lift up started to unroll. Their mouths dropped open as the canvas rolled back to reveal a stiff and discolored human hand.

LeSeur's eyes darted from the women to Phil as they edged away from the canvas. He narrowed his eyes, trying to assess the situation. "Is ... this a joke?"

"No, no, this is no joke," Phil said, looking shocked and a little green. "I'm pretty sure we didn't leave *that* in here for the winter." He clapped his hand over his mouth as he barked out a laugh and then gasped as the full impact of what they were looking at hit him.

LeSeur stepped up to the canvas. "I swear, Phil, if this is a joke ..." He looked up at the other man. "Nope, I thought not. Well, I guess it's going to take a lot longer to put up the Tent now." He shook his head, pointing at the two women. "Don't move. No, you, Deb, get your husbands to guard the door. Tell them, no one in or out. But don't tell anyone anything yet, please." He looked toward Pat and Phil. "And you two just stand still so we can keep the crime scene as clean as possible." He sighed deeply and grumbled, "As if *that's* going to happen. Only about a hundred people have tramped over this mud today. Oh, this is going to be *real* easy." LeSeur's brow furrowed in a way that Pat remembered from the previous year when the last dead body had been found.

Deb ran out the door, holding her stomach with both hands. Closing the door firmly behind her, she thought, *To think I gave up a tennis match to be here!*

For one brief moment, there was silence. The sun had broken through the clouds, and sunlight streamed in through the small row of windows on the side wall. Pat glanced around the barn at the stacked boxes that held the props, keeping her gaze anywhere but on that hand.

If I had just stayed in the chalet to warm up the lunch, Pat thought, shivering a little, *I could be drinking coffee right now. Please, Lord, don't let us get hooked into another murder investigation.* She felt her body begin to sway, and she did her best not to move, hoping against hope that her balancing exercises would help her.

Looking up and spying Pat, LeSeur growled, "You and your friend have the strangest habit of showing up around dead bodies. And just to be clear … you will not try solving this one, right?"

Pat remembered well her last encounter with LeSeur when their paths crossed during a murder investigation of a patron from the Black Cat Coffeehouse.

At that moment LeSeur spied Sam, snapping another photo. "And get that damn camera out of this barn. This isn't a Big Top show! This is a crime scene!"

Sam sheepishly lowered his camera and backed out of the barn.

LeSeur turned his attention back to Pat. "You're clear on what I said?"

Pat solemnly nodded her head as she held her hand over her nose and mouth, trying not to breathe too deeply. The smell of the body filled the room. "Of course," she said, her voice muffled. "You can count on it."

Though she really meant it at the time, no less true words had ever been spoken. In her wildest imagination, and she had one, she couldn't have dreamed up what happened next. Or the circumstances that presented themselves that would pull her and her best friend into danger. No, Detective LeSeur was not going to be a happy camper.

Chapter Three

That same day, the phone rang at the home of county coroner Ruth Epstein. Ruth answered, listened attentively, and then tossed her cell phone on the kitchen table. "Why is it always cold and rainy when I get called to a scene outside?" she grumbled to her husband, Joel.

Joel grunted sympathetically from behind his *New York Times*. "Well, at least it's not the middle of the night." It still amazed him that his petite gray-haired wife didn't mind being around dead bodies. He shuddered and then smiled, reminding himself that she was equally amazed by his work—that he could deal with messy divorces and court cases and sleep through the night was beyond her comprehension.

"Car accident?" he asked, peering over his paper.

"Nope," Ruth called from the hall as she put on her boots and picked up her bag. "Where is my rain hat?"

"I think it's in the front closet. Let me get it for you."

Joel left his paper regretfully. It was such a luxury to read it all the way through on a Sunday afternoon. He turned to their dog that had gotten up from under the table. "Come on, Sydney, let's get Mom's hat, and then I'll take you for that walk she promised you."

The dog wagged his tail, as if he knew exactly what Joel had said, and put in a bark for good measure. Joel retrieved Ruth's hat and brought it to her as she opened the back door to leave.

"We have film society movie night at Stage North," he reminded her, "and we're signed up to sell tickets and make popcorn."

She smiled at him. "Better plan on going on your own. This one is a body at the Tent. Can you believe it?" She gave him a kiss on the cheek. "I'll call. Love you." Out the door she went, her mind already the twenty-five miles down the road and an infinity away from her home life.

Joel grabbed his jacket and stepped out onto the porch, with Sydney close on his heels. He pulled the door closed, and they set off on their walk. *Maybe I'll call Bob to help me at Stage North,* he thought. "Come on, Syd, get a move on!"

Ruth took a deep breath, like an actress coming onto the stage, and stepped into the barn at the bottom of the ski hill. She willed herself to focus. Just inside the barn door, she stopped, her razor-sharp mind taking in the whole scene. The police had already set up bright lights. Two uniformed officers, their breath visible in the chilly barn, were standing just inside the door, waiting for her.

Ruth stuffed her driving gloves into her coat pocket

as she mentally divided the room into sections. The door area had a dirt floor, trampled by many volunteers' feet. To the left, shelves were filled with pile upon pile of dusty props and costumes, reminding her of a Victorian attic, full of forgotten treasures. To her right, rolls of canvases were left where they had been when the workers had been forced to stop. Beside them sat a wooden chair, as if waiting for an occupant. And there, on the ground among the canvases, was the body.

"Somebody have a heart attack putting up the Tent, Sal?" she asked as she shook the young deputy's hand. Even as she asked, Ruth realized that couldn't be the case. For one thing, there was no emergency medical unit on the scene, and for another, she knew that musty smell. Violent death, even in the cold, had its own aroma, and she recognized it in the barn.

Sal shook his head. "No, this one's been here a while. But that's your job. You tell me." He crossed his arms.

"Well, now, did you find it in among these canvases? Don't give me that look," she added after noticing Sal's defiant posture. "I know that you know enough not to move a body. Let's see what I can give you. I'm not a character in one of those detective novels Pat and Deb threaten to write—you know, someone who has all the answers—but I'll give you what I can now. The rest you'll have to wait for until the autopsy."

Ruth set down her bag, pulled on a pair of latex gloves, and dabbed some Vicks into her nose. "But thanks for the warning about how long the body's been here. Let the games begin." She took a few cautious steps toward the body, carefully watching where she walked through the crime scene area. "It looks like you've started without me," she said, glancing disapprovingly at Sal over her glasses.

Sal raised his hands, as if to ward off her judgmental

look. "Now, Ruth, we haven't touched the body, except for when they first found it. LeSeur was one of the volunteers on the scene, if you can believe it." He rubbed his chin. "All I've done is get the volunteers out of the building and lay down some strips of tape on the ground so we can go over every inch when you're done." He tipped his soggy fishing hat in her direction. "Strictly by the book."

Ruth nodded. "I'll want to talk to LeSeur and who-ever found the body. You know I like to be thorough. Where should I walk?" she asked, pulling out her little Canon and snapping pictures.

Sal pointed to a path that had been taped off in the mud. Ruth nodded again and handed her overcoat to a dep-uty. She approached her job as she did everything in her life, with quiet consideration and astute methodology.

Stopping a few feet from the canvas that still held the body, Ruth carefully looked at the way the body was lying halfway out of the large blue canvas. She snapped a few more photos at a different angle.

"Hey, Salvadore, was the body rolled up or found like this?"

"Rolled up. They found it when they tried to lift the canvas."

"Dead weight, you might say," snickered one of the other deputies.

Ruth turned slowly to look at him. "Kid, I know we haven't worked on any cases together before, so I will tell you this for the first and last time: I don't like 'dead' jokes, and I don't ever tolerate jokes about my dead clients. This person is somebody's child. Someone is probably worried about him right now. Every time you are in a situation like this, I want you to think, 'What if this was my dad? How would I like him to be treated?'" Shaking her head she turned back to the body. "Enough said. I won't mention it again."

Already her focus was on the scene. Everyone waiting at the door faded away as Ruth's love of the mystery of life and death took over. She pressed the button on her hand-held micro-recorder—a gift from Joel, who knew his wife so well—and spoke softly. "This is Ruth Epstein, and it's May 20 at 1:10 p.m., at the Chautauqua tent site outbuilding. The scene has been trampled by many volunteers, and currently the body is half out of a tent canvas. Detective Sal Burrows, the officer in charge from Bayfield County, has said it was found rolled up with all the canvases, which had been put away for the winter."

She moved closer and squatted down. *I'm getting too old for this,* she thought as her knees creaked. She continued her spiel into the recorder. "The body is lying face down, but the position may have been altered because the workers tried to move the canvas. The building is unheated and appears to have been cold and dry all winter, which may have contributed to the body's lack of decomposition."

Ruth took a pen from her pocket and used it to gently pull away part of the canvas. "Subject is male, about six feet tall and dressed in jeans, a sweater, and western-style boots. A cursory check shows no visible wounds." As she pulled away the rest of the canvas, the corpse moved slightly, causing the gathering behind her to gasp. Ruth didn't bother to look around; she just called out, "Sal, I need two guys to turn him over."

Everyone instantly looked away or down at their feet, as if they were school children, thinking that if they didn't look up, the teacher wouldn't call on them.

"For goodness sake!" Ruth said exasperatedly. "Sal, get some gloves out of my bag and come help me!"

Sal sheepishly came forward and gently tugged on the canvas, but the body didn't move. Ruth stood up, turning off her recorder.

"Okay," she said, "on the count of three. One ... two ... three." The body rolled over. "Thank you." She looked up and noticed Sal's white face. "Stay if you want," she said without rancor. "Just remember, if you start to faint, fall away from the body." To Sal's credit, he stayed.

Ruth turned her recorder back on. "We have turned the body over, and there is obvious damage to the head, a striking blow, probably with a blunt object or tool. It looks like the nose is crushed in and also the left eye. No other discernable wounds that I can see. There is a large amount of dried bloodstains covering the face and top clothing. If the deceased was put in the canvases when the Tent was taken down, that would make him here about ..." She paused, silently counting the months in her head. "Five months." Ruth no longer heard anything other than her own voice as she continued to describe the scene and the body.

Just who are you, Mr. Corpse? she thought, interrupting her dictation and reaching in his pocket for more clues to his identity.

At the same time, outside the nearby chalet, Deb was shifting her weight nervously from foot to foot. "Why is it always hurry up and wait?" she pouted. "I'm hungry! The least they could do is feed us after all that work."

"Settle down, Deb. We want them to get this right. This is a horrible thing that has happened," Pat said sagely, glancing over at the young deputy who kept watch over the long line of people waiting to be called for questioning.

"But we've stood here for over an hour *after* they herded us into line like a bunch of animals," Deb grumbled.

"I know, Deb, but we want to cooperate. *We* know we

didn't do anything wrong. So it's just a nuisance, that's all," Pat soothed.

"But why were Mitch and Marc fingerprinted first? They weren't even in the barn!" Deb whined. "My favorite part of the tent-raising is the potluck feast we have for lunch afterwards," she added petulantly, trying to solicit a little sympathy. When she didn't get a response, she turned her attention toward the chalet, from which Mitch and Marc were emerging, each with a satisfied smile. Marc carried a Mountain Dew, and Mitch, a Diet Coke.

"What did you bring me?" Deb called out.

"How was it, Mitch? Did they ask any questions?" Sam's voice interrupted apprehensively from behind her.

"Let me see your fingers," Carl Carlson ordered impolitely. "I want to see what kind of ink stains it leaves. I've never been fingerprinted before."

"I have," replied Mitch enigmatically.

"When were you fingerprinted before?" Deb asked, although she looked quizzically at Pat.

"Does it hurt?" asked Carl.

"Nothing to it, guys," Marc replied, holding up his perfectly clean fingers. "Especially since none of us had anything to do with this."

"Just a precaution; that's what they said," Mitch added.

"What's going to happen to all that food in there?" Deb asked longingly.

"I thought you two had turned over a new leaf about food," Marc teased.

Deb blushed, like a kid caught with her hand in the cookie jar. "Sure, we've done better. But I have hypoglycemia, you know—low blood sugar. And when I'm under stress, it's worse."

"And this is a big one," Pat said, coming to her friend's rescue.

"Don't let it get to you so much," Marc said, trying to offer comfort. "See you at home. We're cleared to leave."

"Bye, you two. We have to go," Mitch added. "We're stopping at Patsy's on the way home for a burger."

"Do you mind starting dinner tonight?" Deb called, glaring at the two men as they walked down the stairs to the car. "The way this is going we'll be here until midnight! Hey! Give me that Mountain Dew!" she barked after them. Marc just waved and kept on going.

"I can't believe they wouldn't let us finish hauling the bleachers out of the barn," grumbled someone behind them.

Pat turned around and rallied a smile. "It's okay, Phil. Somehow this baby of yours will be safely delivered on time," she soothed.

"Pat Kerrey! Next!" Sal called impatiently from the screen door of the chalet.

"Good things come to those who wait," Sam teased Deb. "Especially those who wait patiently."

"Tell him to pick me next," Deb urged Pat as she made her way to the front of the line.

"I'm not going to stand in line when there's so much work to be done!" Phil complained loudly. He turned and stomped off toward the big tent. "If they need me, they know where to find me! I've got a show to get out."

He's going to get in trouble, Deb thought.

Deb crept to the screen door, trying to peek inside.

A young officer stepped in front of her, blocking her view of the interior. "Can I help you, ma'am?" he inquired politely.

"Just ... looking for the bathroom," Deb replied.

"Sorry, but no one goes in until they're called," he replied firmly. Then, with a twinkle in his eye, he said, "Really, Deb. You should know where the restrooms are by now."

Pat's unmistakable voice rang out just then. "Just don't mess up my fingernails. I don't want to ruin my new manicure."

Deb smiled, her mood lightened by Pat's silliness.

Half an hour later, Pat sat in the Adirondack chair outside the chalet, jiggling her foot impatiently. *Maybe I should get in the warm car. What on earth is taking so long?*

Only a few people remained waiting outside.

A minute later, Deb emerged from the chalet, a sheepish look on her face.

"What did they do to you in there?" Pat asked. "I was ready to send in a search party! I thought maybe they put you to work or something."

"Worse than that," Deb replied, holding up her hands. Her fingers were covered with sooty ink, and her hands looked as if she had been cleaning chimneys. There were handprints on her sweater and a few on her face.

"What the—?" Pat asked.

"They must have made me roll my fingers at least twenty times. First, I kept messing up when they got to the middle finger, so they had to start the whole process over … and over … and over," she complained. "Then, when they finally got a full set of prints, they showed the card to LeSeur. He took one look and told Sal they had to do it again. Then it took another six tries to get a full set again." "You're kidding!" Pat said incredulously.

"I *so* wish I were!" Deb wailed. "After three times like that, LeSeur finally declared me a non-person. He said I don't have *any* fingerprints,"

"What do you mean, you don't have prints?"

"When they couldn't see any of those little whirls on the paper, they asked me what I did for work. Turns out, my stint as a nurse all those years ago and all that hand-washing with abrasive soap destroyed all the lines!" Deb said.

"Did you grab any food while you were in there?" Pat asked.

"Nope. Marc's making dinner, remember? Let's get going."

"Look on the bright side, Deb," Pat said playfully as the two women walked to their car. "We have a contact at the CIA. When you're ready for your next career change, you can just call up Andy Ross, and maybe you can be a spy!"

"Very funny, Pat," Deb replied as she drove out of the parking lot, eagerly anticipating Marc's dinner.

"Watch out for the speed-cop!" Pat said as they turned the corner onto the highway to Ashland.

Later that same night, clean and dry at last, Deb, Marc, Pat, and Mitch sat in the dining room on Chapple Avenue, enjoying the soft glow of candlelight as they unwound from the tensions of the day. The salad was fresh spinach and strawberry marinated in balsamic vinegar. Deb bit into a fresh-picked Bayfield strawberry, savoring the juicy taste. Marc had outdone himself once again; he had whipped up a memorable and tasty meal, like Mickey the magician, conjuring the dancing broom and bucket—except that Marc's meals never seemed to go awry.

"M-m-m ... this is so good. It's all too good!" Pat said appreciatively, biting into a warm slice of beer-herb bread. "How did you have time to bake bread today?"

"Deb made it yesterday on her day off," Marc replied,

smiling proudly in Deb's direction.

"It's a Linberg favorite," Deb said. "It never fails."

"Anyone ready for next course?" Marc asked.

Clearing the table, as his parents had taught him to do with company, Marc then brought in a big bowl of ratatouille and a platter of grilled chicken.

"Oh, Marc, you sure know the way to my heart," Pat sighed. "I just love ratatouille."

"It's not very good this time," Marc apologized. "I had to buy tomatoes and zucchini at the co-op. It's nothing like picking them right from the garden."

"Stop it, you silly boy!" Deb admonished. "Do not apologize for your food—ever!"

"All food is good that someone else cooks, especially when that someone is you," Pat chimed in.

"Mitch did the chicken!" Marc said, trying to deflect attention from his wife's gentle rebuke.

"Grilled to perfection," Deb said.

"He may not be able to cook much, but he sure can do chicken on the grill," Marc agreed.

Mitch blushed at the praise. "Just wait until dessert! I did that, too."

Lifting her glass, Deb toasted, "Here's to the cooks!"

"And here's to a good ending to a very terrible day," Pat added.

"Speaking of that," Marc said sternly, and the lightness of the previous moment suddenly vanished, "you two are going to stay at least a mile away from this thing, right?"

"What do you mean, 'this thing'?" Deb bristled. "You're talking about a dead person, probably a murdered person. You do understand the seriousness of it all, don't you?"

"Isn't that what I've just been telling you?" Marc asked defensively.

"One thing we do hope you are serious about is keeping yourselves safe," Mitch pitched in, looking lovingly at Pat.

Deb smiled as she noticed Mitch admiring Pat's new lithe body. *Married twenty years, and he still has a sparkle in his eye,* Deb thought.

"Remember what happened the last time you two got caught up in something like this?" Marc lectured. "You almost got killed up in that crazy artist's apartment, remember?"

"Of course we remember!" Pat answered, "*We* were there, remember?"

"Past is not always prologue to the future," Deb said wearily.

Pat turned to Marc. "How long do you think that body was in that barn, anyway?"

"Depends," Marc answered. "If the temperature stays cold, a dead body can be preserved for several months without decomposing. My guess is that it was probably there since last fall."

"Really?" the two women answered in stereo.

"I think it's time for dessert!" Mitch interrupted, trying to escape the unpleasant table talk. "Anyone for ice cream?"

"Sure, I'll have some," Marc eagerly replied. "And then I would love some help getting my boat uncovered so I can give it a bath before we launch it."

Chapter Four

Bright and early on Monday morning, Deb took out her German coffee press from the cupboard. She scooped three heaping tablespoons of freshly ground coffee into the bottom and then slowly poured boiling water over the top to the two-cup line of the glass jar. She inserted the mesh plunger over the hot water and slowly pressed the metal toward the bottom of the flask, marveling at how the color of the water quickly changed from clear to deep chocolate. She had learned about coffee presses after visiting her German-exchange daughter's home in Germany a few years before.

Deb kicked off her shoes and made her way to the couch, taking a steaming mug of the freshly brewed Traveler's Blend. *How appropriate*, she thought as she inhaled the fresh aroma. Deb caught her reflection in the hallway mirror and noticed how thin her face looked. Her husband, Marc, was already relaxing in the living room, enjoying a rare moment of quiet, engrossed in a medical mystery novel.

"Hon, can you believe it's been a whole year since Pat and I returned from our trip to Nevis?" she asked dreamily, joining him on the couch.

"Oh, boy. I know that look," Marc replied with a sigh. He put his finger in the book to hold his spot. "You're starting to get that wanderlust again, aren't you?"

Deb felt a stirring of desire deep down in her soul, but it wasn't for carnal pleasure. *God knows I get plenty of that with Marc*, she thought, and she giggled to herself as she sipped her coffee. *Hot!* she thought, *and not just the coffee.* She companionably nudged Marc's shoulder with her own and giggled again as he looked at her quizzically. Her spirit of adventure was churning inside like a funnel, stirring up dust in her life and clouding her view of the present moment.

Marc glanced over at her with a knowing look.

"I am so lucky that you tolerate my wanderlust so well," Deb said gratefully.

"It's only taken me twenty-five years of marriage to learn certain things," he joked. "You require a certain quota of new sights and travel to old and new places in order to feel complete."

"At least I'm not a travel addict the way our sister-in-law is," Deb retorted. "Your brother's wife doesn't consider it a complete month unless she's going off alone to some exotic locale for a few days. What a life that would be!"

"Where does that travel bug come from, anyway?" Marc wondered aloud.

"For me, it has to be from my great-grandma Agnes McKinney. She's the one who, at thirteen years of age, climbed onto a covered wagon with shirt-tail relatives and made the long and arduous journey from New Jersey to the Kansas prairie in 1809. She was married four times, you know. She lived for a time in a sod house, outlived all of her husbands, and died in her nineties, a content woman," Deb related.

30

"Here's to Grandma Agnes' spirit!" Marc agreed, raising his can of Mountain Dew. "And to no more husbands!"

Snuggling in on the couch helped Deb to briefly escape her ruminations about finding a dead body. She took stock of the changes that had happened in the past year since her trip to the Caribbean island of Nevis with Pat. Deb reflected that one constant in the past year—other than her marriage to Marc—was the steady presence of Pat, her best friend for thirty-five years. A year before, Pat and Mitchell had decided to have a respite from city life and had purchased an old Victorian, one block away from Deb and Marc.

What fun it's been to walk with Pat to the local Curves each morning, Deb thought, *and then to the Black Cat Coffeehouse after our workout. Forty pounds lighter and no more achy knees on the stairs! It has been a good thing—a really good thing!*

As Marc returned to his reading, Deb's thoughts were interrupted by the beeping of her phone, which that indicated she had a message. Julia had returned from her year's stay in Madrid as an exchange student and was safely enrolled at the University of Wisconsin in Madison. "Hon, it's a message from Julia. She got a ride home from school after finals!" Deb said excitedly to Marc.

"Umm," Marc replied, not really listening. She took another sip of her coffee.

Deb missed having Julia and all her friends in the house. Luckily, their household had been unexpectedly blessed by the arrival of a ray of sunshine from Paraguay, in the form of Bruno, their most recent exchange student. Deb, Marc, and their son, Eric, had chosen Bruno from the biographies sent to them by Ruth Epstein, who also served as regional leader for the local student-exchange program.

Deb and Marc had been fairly certain that Bruno would be a good fit with their family, particularly Eric. After all, Bruno played soccer and tennis, and he was musical, just like Eric.

"Isn't it fun having a persistently happy boy who sings all the time, is helpful to a T, and whose magnetic personality and charisma draw a steady stream of kids here?" Deb asked.

"A lot easier than our own kids," Marc answered from behind his book.

Almost on cue, Deb and Marc's moment of serenity was interrupted by the sound of pounding hooves on the front stairway. Eric and Bruno appeared, looking scruffy and unshaven, clearly relishing their day off school. "Hey, Mom, what's for lunch?" Bruno teased.

"How am I going to survive the rest of this year with a second growing teenage boy in the house?" Deb teased back. "And lunch is whatever you can find in the fridge."

The boys wandered amiably into the kitchen and shut the door behind them, whispering conspiratorially.

"Isn't this a dream come true?" Deb asked Marc for perhaps the hundredth time. "I'm so glad we got to take Bruno to Montana and Washington DC since he's been here. Can you believe that it's already almost time for our annual summer pilgrimage to the Jersey shore?"

"Is this a rhetorical question, or do you really want an answer?" Marc asked good-naturedly, glancing up at her from his book.

"Really, Marc, I'm already dreading his leaving ... although not very much because that would violate my new-found priority of living in the moment." She sighed heavily. "Truth be known, I just don't know how we will survive the parting and the farewell to Bruno at the end of June."

"Just enjoy every minute of what's left," Marc wisely responded. "And make sure that you keep enough Mountain Dew and snacks at home."

"Don't you think Eric just loves having a big brother for the first time in his life? He's my baby, for heaven's sake, and look how mature and responsible he's becoming," Deb sniffed.

"Sure," Marc agreed. "That kid is lucky enough to just float through life with ease."

Deb seemed to be relaxed, sipping her fresh brew, but she suddenly turned to Marc and blurted out, "I want to go to Paraguay!"

"Paraguay?" Marc responded apprehensively, putting down his book.

"It's now at the top of my list of travel destinations. The pull is strong," Deb said dreamily.

"That's not likely to happen any time soon," Marc responded, inserting a tone of realism into Deb's fantasy.

Deb sighed again and put her dream for more travel out to the universe, as she had put so many other dreams and desires of her heart. *It'll happen*, she thought.

Deb glanced down at her watch and jumped up. "I would love to sit here and daydream with you a while longer, but I need to call the office and let them know I probably won't be in today. I have to call Kris and ask her to set up an appointment for me. I have a court trial coming up next week."

"The glamorous life of a divorce lawyer! Not another of those crazy custody battles, is it?" Marc asked sympathetically. "Those drain you so much. I don't know how you keep working with all those broken people."

"Believe it or not, some of my clients are truly interested in improving their lives and receiving good service," Deb responded, "even if many of them seem indifferent or ungrateful or just so beaten down that they can't see their way clear out of the darkness."

"Don't you ever feel like you're wasting your time?"

"Of course I do. That's why I have all this nagging

doubt about whether to continue. I just keep trying to be a torch-bearer, but sometimes it's just impossible to lead people who refuse to take off their blinders."

Marc reached over and squeezed her hand. "Go get 'em, my dear light woman!"

Deb walked into the kitchen and dialed the office on her cell phone. "Hi, Kris," she said loudly, over the laughter of teenage boys. "Sorry, but Marc and the boys are home today, and I'm not coming in. You can give out my cell number if someone really needs to reach me. I need a mental-health day. I want you to call the Thompsons and schedule an appointment with them to meet with me."

"*Together?*" Kris answered, the surprise clearly audible in her voice.

"Not on your life!" Deb replied. "Be sure that they don't even get a chance to see each other coming and going, either. And thanks. You're a lifesaver."

Deb snapped her phone shut and noticed the *Ashland Daily Press* lying open on the kitchen table. The headline caught her eye: *Death at the Tent*.

She continued reading:

> *Local and regional patrons of Lake Superior Big Top Chautauqua were stunned to learn on Sunday of a grizzly discovery at their beloved Big Top.*
>
> *The body of an unidentified male was discovered in a roll of canvas on Sunday during the annual tent-raising. Due to inclement weather, the tent-raising had been postponed from Saturday until Sunday.*

"We went to lift the roll, found it to be heavy, and out fell a hand," said Phil Anich, operations manager for the Tent.

Neither the name of the deceased nor the manner of death has been released by authorities. Sal Burrows, Bayfield County Sheriff's Department detective, is in charge of the investigation. He had no comment.

"This is a horrible event, no doubt," said Carl Carlson, president of the board of directors for Chautauqua. "But the spirit of Chautauqua is strong. This tent show has endured many other tragedies in the past and will surely survive this one. The show will go on."

Carlson has asked that anyone with any information should contact the Bayfield County Sheriff's Department. "We have no further comment at this time. The Chautauqua organization will fully cooperate with the investigation," Carlson commented.

Lake Superior Big Top Chautauqua produces and presents a summer season of concerts, plays, and lectures, and a highly acclaimed professional local troupe, which performs original multimedia musicals in the Tent and on tour. The three-month summer schedule includes performances by renowned national, regional, and touring musicians. Opening night is scheduled for this Thursday evening.

Finishing her cup of coffee and feeling restless, Deb decided to walk Strider, her golden retriever, and to stop to see Pat. Despite her thoughts and fantasies of travel, Deb just couldn't stop thinking about the dead body that had been found in the canvas at the Big Top. She wondered how the poor soul had ended up hidden in that barn for so long without being missed.

At the same time as Deb was walking Strider, Sal Burrows and Gary LeSeur were sitting on either side of a desk in the sheriff's office, discussing the discovery of the dead body.

"Technically, the coroner is calling it a death by a blunt instrument, used with great force directly to the face. Can't she just tell me what it was and whether or not it was murder? Jeez Louise, why did I ever take this freaking job in the first place? I could have stayed with you in Ashland. But no, I wanted to be in charge of my own place. Well, this is working out *real* well! Two weeks into the job in Bayfield County, a place where, need I remind you, they assured me nothing ever happens, and I'm trying to figure out how a six- to eight-month-old decomposing body could have gotten into our major tourist attraction! The mayor has called me six times, and don't even ask how many times Phil has called. Who murdered him? We don't even know who it is yet. Help." The young detective looked as bad as he sounded as he slumped down in his new chair.

"Calm down, Sally," LeSeur said soothingly. "No one expects you to solve it in five minutes. You're going to do great, and now that the okay has come down, we can do this together." He patted his young former deputy on the shoulder sympathetically.

"But what do we do?" Sal wailed, slamming down his coffee cup.

"Settle," his former boss said a little bit more firm-ly. "First, we have already done a lot. We've secured the scene, had the coroner in, and talked to the volunteers who were helping yesterday. And we can safely say 'murder' be-cause no dead person ever accidentally rolled himself up in a piece of eight-by-ten-foot tent canvas." He took a breath and relaxed his shoulders—the yoga technique that Deb had taught his wife surely did help him, too, even though he didn't want her to know.

"Right," the younger man said, leaning forward on the desk. "So what now?"

"Now, we roll up our sleeves and get to work. And as much as I shudder at the thought, we bring in those two women who discovered the body and find out what they remember."

"You mean ...? Oh, no! Those two are like melting choc-olate—they stick to everything. Oh, why did I take this job?"

Growling, LeSeur stood up and handed Sal the phone. "Call Deb first," he instructed. "She's the saner of the two. And stop whining. Take it like a man. After all, they did give you a dollar-fifty-an-hour raise."

Grinning, Sal picked up the phone directory to look for the number. "Hey, Suzie," he called into the next room, "can you bring us another pot of coffee? I think we're going to need it."

Chapter Five

Pat got up even earlier than usual on Monday morning and went out on her side deck. She had made herself a pot of Sister's Choice coffee. Sunday had been a long day and an even longer night after discovering the body. She still didn't know who it was—the Tent's gossip mill hadn't reached her yet. Even though it was a sunny day, Pat shivered as she remembered the scene. It was as if cold fingers were running up her spine. She zipped up her black workout jacket a little farther and sat at the ancient wooden table in the sun. *What a circus it was after the discovery!* she thought. She sat down, poured herself her first cup—adding plenty of cream—and sighed as she replayed the events in her head.

After we found the body—no! Not just a "body." It's a person, someone's son or husband—everything was such a blur of people and noise and lights. But Ruth arrived within an hour of the discovery.

Just then, Ruth walked by the side deck with Sydney,

her Australian sheepdog.

"Hi, Ruth! Wasn't that just an awful scene?" Pat called out. Ruth waved, then walked up to the deck. As she approached, Pat asked, "How on earth did you get involved in that anyway? Bayfield isn't your usual territory."

Ruth nodded. "Unfortunately for me, the coroner from Bayfield County is on a kayak trip out in the Apostle Islands and won't be available for another week or so." Ruth's reply was pleasant enough, but her eyes were filled with unanswered questions about why she had met Pat and Deb at yet another crime scene.

"At least I didn't go outside and throw up after seeing the body," Pat said, remembering the horror of the moment and shaking her head. "I wanted to, though. And what a good thing that LeSeur just happened to be on the scene. Is he going to stay involved in the investigation?"

"Technically, it is not his beat," Ruth answered, "but Sal Burrows sure was glad that LeSeur was there. He readily admitted to me that he needs the help—welcomes it from his old boss at the Ashland P.D. But you should have seen the look he had when he told me that you and Deb were there too!" She laughed, remembering. "His face was celery-green!"

"Can't really blame him," said Pat. "Since his only other murder investigation in his entire career had Deb and me woven into it like pieces in a rag rug." She sighed heavily. "I am just so exhausted. And I'm wondering what will happen now, after all that work getting the Tent ready for opening night. Do you think New First Night will happen on time?"

"As far as I'm concerned, the on-site investigation is over. Of course, the building will be cordoned off, but that shouldn't be a problem," Ruth replied. "Now it's up to the crew to decide if they can pull off the first few shows."

"I don't know much about the financing of that big tent, but I know they try to keep all expenses to a minimum and that every show counts," Pat said. "After all, that's why so many people like us volunteer to park cars and sell T-shirts or raffle tickets."

"Oh, by the way, Pat," Ruth said. "My catching you like this has saved me a call—Linda and Forrest had asked me to call you."

Pat's eyes widened in amazement. "Call me? Whatever for?"

Ruth lowered her voice and explained, "This isn't public knowledge yet, but the body found in the canvas was Monty McIntyre."

"Mac? Good Lord! How awful!"

"Linda said that she and Forrest were sometimes members of the church you're serving. She would like you to help with some kind of service."

Pat nodded woodenly, still a bit shocked. "How did you find out?"

"ID in his pocket," Ruth replied.

"Oh. Of course. But when can we expect to plan a funeral?" Pat inquired.

"Well, it's going to be a while before the body is released. It's pretty clear that it wasn't an accident that killed Mac. I'll let you know when I know," Ruth said.

"I'll give Linda a call, but if you talk to her before I do, tell her I'll be glad to help out in any way I can. The poor woman."

Ruth's dog pulled impatiently on his leash. "I've got to get going, Pat. I have a lot of calls to make today. Talk to you soon."

"See you later, Ruth," Pat said as her neighbor started toward home, with Sydney's stump of a tail waggling eagerly beside her.

Pat shook her hair and then ran her fingers through it, as if she could shake off last night. She took another sip of her coffee, admiring the cup. *I hope Marc can make a few more of these,* she thought. *The girls are coming up from the cities, so I'll need them.* Marc had made a set of coffee cups for her birthday last July and had promised two more and a sugar and creamer next. *It's great having a best friend whose husband's hobby is potting.*

Pat stretched out her legs, placing her feet up on the bench across from her. She took a long swallow and looked around. *Let's see,* she mused, *the peonies need to be decapitated. Yesterday's storm really devastated them. But except for a few branches down, everything else looks okay. At least the weeds haven't totally taken over the flowerbeds.* Glancing down to the cobblestone patio below her, Pat saw what looked like a small forest taking root in between the bricks. She sighed. She loved her maple trees—they towered over the three-story Victorian home and nicely shaded the table on the deck—but she was not fond of the "spinner babies" that fell from the trees in the spring and lodged in places they didn't belong. They grew everywhere, even in the rain gutters. And Pat felt like a murderer, plucking out the sturdy green plants and tossing them in the compost pile. "Helicopters," her son Martin used to call them, she remembered fondly, as she bit into a bakery scone.

How did they manage to make these so good? she thought, momentarily distracted from her inventory of yard work. The scones seemed especially wonderful, now that she limited herself to only one or two a week. Still, being healthier was worth it. Pat wiped her fingers on her napkin. *Whatever you call them—helicopters or weeds—I have to get them up before they take over the patio. If only I didn't hear ghostly little tree screams in my mind as I pull them up.*

"Better get back to work," she told herself. Humming, she started weeding. After half an hour of swatting at flies and sweating in spite of the breeze, Pat realized she was holding a handful of weeds and staring off in the distance, wondering what Deb was doing. Until recently, she would have picked up the coffee pot and cup, walked down the block, gone through Deb's back door and into the kitchen, and peeked out onto the porch to see if Deb was finished with her yoga. Now the alpha house was filled with male hormones, and she avoided it. Their two husbands joked that "the girls" could get along without them easier than without each other.

"Still ..." Pat groaned as she got up from her knees. She surveyed all the little trees sticking up their heads among the bricks and then noticed the puny pile she had managed to pull. "It's a top-of-the-morning, beautiful Wisconsin May day," she said gaily to the birds who were watching her. "And I'm not going to waste it pulling weeds." With a flourish, she tossed the pile in the compost heap, brushed the dirt off of her jeans, and started to sing with forced gaiety, ignoring her aching knees. "Oh, what a beautiful morning! Oh, what a beautiful day. I've got a beautiful feeling ... everything's going my way!"

"Who's singing?" a voice rang out from next door.

"Oh, hi, Terri," Pat called to her neighbor. "Come on over. I've got coffee." Pat went back up on the deck to pour a second cup for herself and a new one for Terri. She always kept an extra cup on hand in case a neighbor stopped by.

"You sound so perky this morning!" Terri exclaimed, taking the proffered cup from Pat's outstretched hand.

"No matter how much I sing or how loud I sing it, that is not how I am really feeling," Pat replied honestly.

"Why? Is something wrong?" Terri asked.

Pat shrugged. *What is it I am feeling?* she wondered as she slathered the last bite of her scone with homemade raspberry jam.

"Is something wrong at work?" Terri prodded.

"No. It's just part-time interim work at the Lutheran church. It's all going fine. That church will be a fine place for some young pastor and family," Pat answered. "No, it's not that. It's—" Pat was momentarily startled by a banging noise coming from the second floor of her house.

"You entertaining strangers in your house again?" Terri teased.

"Not this time," Pat joked. "Mitchell's up from the city early this week. He'll be here for a whole week instead of just the weekend. And I'm glad."

"Do you miss him when he's gone?" Terri asked.

"Sure. But since our townhouse in the city hasn't sold yet, we just have to put up with his working where the pay is better." *Nope, that's not what I'm feeling,* Pat decided. She looked over the edge of the deck at the patio, half-cleared of its tiny forest, and let out a wry laugh. "I haven't the slightest interest in getting down to finish that job. And it's not because my knees and back hurt."

"So what's the beef?" Terri persisted, leaning closer to Pat. "Is it the death at the Tent?"

"Ah-h. Is it the death at the Tent," Pat repeated. "Boy, that sure isn't helping my mood." She shook her head and added emphatically, "But I'm *not* getting involved."

"Good luck with that," Terri replied amiably. "Gotta go, Pat. Thanks for the coffee. And keep singing!"

Pat waved good-bye as Terri ambled back to her own yard.

So, Pat, what is it you are feeling? Drumming her fingers on the table, she delved a little deeper into her thoughts. After all, wasn't that what she told people to do when they came in for counseling? *"What would your feeling be if you knew what it was?"* Or *"Make a list of what you feel, and then explain each item."* *Stupid*, she chided herself. *Why do I use such stupid techniques? Yet ...*

44

"Woof!" Her thoughts were interrupted by the sound of barking. Strider started pulling on his leash once he realized that Deb was walking toward Pat's, where treats were guaranteed.

"Yes, Stridy, we'll be there in a minute. Hang on; you're hurting my arm," she said, pulling firmly on the lead. Just as she got the big golden under control, Pachelbel's Canon in D minor came from her coat pocket—the ringtone on her phone.

"Shoot," she mumbled as she fumbled with the leash and her new cell phone at the same time. She finally managed to answer on the third ring. "Hello?" she squeaked, stumbling over the ancient sidewalk pavers in front of Pat's house.

"Deb? Is that you?" Without waiting for her response, the voice on the other end of the line continued, "This is Salvadore Burrows, over at Bayfield County Sheriff's Department. What I need is—I mean, what you need to do is—heck, what I'm trying to say is that I need you and Pat to come in and talk about the ... incident at the Tent.

"Incident?" Deb smiled wryly as she stopped in the middle of the sidewalk and tugged on Strider's leash. "I hardly would call a death—a murder—an 'incident.'" Then she took pity on the new young investigator. "Sorry, Sal, but you must admit, he couldn't have rolled himself up in that canvas."

"Yeah, I know. LeSeur has already pointed out that little detail to me. Anyway"—he cleared his throat—"can you two come in? Please?" He sounded more like a schoolboy talking to one of his teachers than the detective in charge of a murder investigation.

"When do you want us to come in? My boys are in tennis now, so I have to be home at three-thirty."

"Well ..." He stopped a moment, and Deb heard him speaking to someone. "LeSeur is here right now. Could you come in now? Or is Pat too busy at church?"

Deb walked up the steps of her best friend's side deck, smiling at Pat, who was now sitting in the sun, dirty and resting from the hard work of weeding.

"Hey, Pat!" Deb called, pointing to her phone. "It's Sal. Do you think you can pull yourself away from your farming and join me on a trip to Washburn? He wants us to come to his office today to talk about the murder."

"I've got to get cleaned up and go to an Altar Guild meeting right now. How about we leave in about an hour or so?"

Deb gave her friend a thumbs-up and then said into the phone, "I think I can safely say she'd be willing to come today. How about an hour and a half?"

"The day is looking up," Pat said, smiling as Deb snapped her phone shut. "I'll call you when my meeting is over. Are we just going to see Sal, or are we going to buy clothes?" Now that the two of them had gotten in shape, clothes shopping had become a delight.

"Maybe we can stop at the Brownstone Center, if we have time. First we need to take care of business, though, and stop at the sheriff's office."

Pat grinned at her friend. *Yes, indeed,* she thought. *The day is definitely looking up.*

Pat ran into the house and quickly changed, but just as she stepped out the front door, the phone rang.

Shoot! she thought, trying to decide whether to answer it. *I almost made it. Maybe the caller will try my number at the church.*

After serving in churches for twenty-five years, Pat knew very well that parish work took up most of her days—and nights, too, when necessary. Usually, she'd hop in her car and rush to the church. But today, in keeping with her "get fit and stay that way, or else" program, she planned to walk to the church—and if she didn't hurry, she would be late.

Lord help the pastor who keeps the Altar Guild waiting! Not answering the phone now, she decided. *But then again, what if someone is in the hospital, or ...?* She opened the door and ran into the kitchen, picking up the receiver just as it went to dial tone. *Probably just someone calling about the church cookbook,* she thought.

Pat had jogged halfway down the street when she realized she hadn't locked her front door. She remembered how shocked she was when she had first seen Deb leave the house without locking her door. Now, a few years later, it seemed normal.

As Pat jogged, she continued to think about her feelings of restlessness. *Let's see ... I certainly don't regret the move. Don't really miss the big city, except for an occasional yearning for Thai food. Am I lonesome?* Now that they were empty-nesters, she and Mitchell had made trips to see the grandbabies in Houston fairly regularly. In fact, they'd recently returned from such a trip. And Jane, their daughter, was only four hours away. *No, it's not that.* Her brow furrowed as she probed the weird feeling, much like feeling like a sore tooth with her tongue.

I'm not unhappy, or lonely, or stressed. With a start, she realized things were going too well! She liked a little mystery of the unknown in her life. *I am, in fact, bored.* Not a feeling she was used to having, to be sure.

But there it was—a kind of restlessness, irritability, and itching on the bottoms of her feet. She reached up and absentmindedly swatted a mosquito from her ear. *Oh, Lord, it's that "everything is too predictable" disease I have every once in a while.* She and Mitch had had fun fixing up the Victorian. It was like playing house, and then, no sooner had she moved in the mishmash of furnishings than she and Deb had become embroiled in last year's murder investigation with Detective LeSeur. *What did you think?* she scolded herself firmly. *That another person would conveniently die just so you could feel that flush of discovery and adventure again?*

Yet now, someone had.

Still, it wouldn't hurt to give poor Sal some help, Pat decided. *Just to be helpful. Not to interfere—no, no. After all, he is new at the job. And it was clear the other night that he is in way over his head.*

Little did Pat know that once again she was headed straight into a southeasterner of a mystery. And Deb was in the boat with her. Soon, they would be paddling for their very lives!

Reaching the church, Pat ran up the stairs two at a time.

Wendy, the office manager-slash-bookkeeper-slash-guardian of the realm, was waiting. "You're late! The Altar Guild is already up in the boardroom." Relenting, she smiled at Pat and held out a cup. "I made you coffee. It's caffeinated," she whispered, as she handed it to Pat, along with some papers, "because you're gonna need it."

"What did I do now?" Pat whined.

Some people were born to be pastors, but Pat wasn't one of them. Her husband said it was a great cosmic joke that God played on her—or maybe on the church.

"Nothing. And that's just the trouble. They want you to talk to the janitor. He keeps moving their boxes, doesn't listen to what they say, and won't help put up the decorations for holidays, et cetera and et cetera."

Pat started up the stairs to the second floor but glanced back over her shoulder and saluted briskly. "Once more into the breach."

"Well!" came an exasperated voice from above. "She's finally here."

Chapter Six

Gossip ran rampant through the Black Cat Coffeehouse.

"You heard, didn't you?" Rick asked in a stage whisper across the front round table. Everyone instinctively leaned in closer.

"Heard what?" Wayne asked. "Are you talking about the new health bill or the conspiracy against the poor?"

"Nah, I'm talking about what happened at the Tent last night."

"Oh, sure, everyone knows a body was found," another customer replied. "Bizarre, isn't it? I wonder if they know who it is yet."

"That's what I'm tryin' to tell you! I heard it from a very reliable source that it was one of the musicians."

"Hah, reliable source, is it?" Wayne scoffed. "I'll bet you've been talking to that Suzie at the station, haven't you?"

"Never you mind who my source is," Rick said indignantly. "Do you want to know who they think it is, or not?"

Carol leaned across the table. "Well, I'd like to know. Tell me, if you don't want to talk to Wayne."

"It's not for sure, you understand. But from what they found in his pockets they think it might be *Mac*. They're checking at all his known addresses now."

"You mean that Canadian, Monty McIntyre?" Carol asked. "Didn't he have a thing going with Linda?"

"A *thing*? Who do you think is Forrest's dad, huh?" Wayne sneered.

"Maybe she just got tired of his coming and going," someone else suggested. "Or maybe the kid just couldn't stand the idea of his being his dad, and ... you know ... did him in."

"What did you mean, exactly, by that remark?" Linda Johnson's voice barked so sharply with anger that it hurt to listen to it.

A hush fell over the table. "Oh, hello," Rick said sheepishly. "I guess we didn't see you come in."

"Obviously not! Or you wouldn't have been maligning me and mine, now would you? You bunch of gossips! I have half a mind to pick up this chair and knock some sense into the lot of you. Don't ever let me hear you talk that way about my son again, or you'll be sorry!"

With that, Linda turned on her heel and stomped out, leaving everyone sitting in silence for once.

Chapter Seven

"That's okay. It's okay."
He sat down on the white wooden chair in the barn and
couldn't keep his eyes from the corner.

It just doesn't seem real, not real at all.
That's the place, where my life was changed forever.
Well ... not just mine, he amended.

But so far I've kept it together.
He mentally applauded himself.
"After all this time it would do no good to turn myself in.
He's already dead."
He reasoned with himself for the hundredth time.
Dead. Then why do I feel so dead?
His body started to shake.

"I won't come in here again.
"I won't," he promised himself firmly.
And yet, sitting in the quiet, he knew he
couldn't help but return.
And keep returning,
as if paying homage, or doing penance.

"It's okay. It's okay," he repeated.
"It's going to be okay,"
he said out loud into the gloom.

Chapter Eight

"I'm home!" Pat sang into the phone, a note of relief in her voice.

"I'll drive," Deb answered. "You change; I'll get the car and pick you up soon. So, did they string you up yet?" Without waiting for Pat's answer, she laughed and turned off the phone.

I love my little white Prius, Deb thought as she slid into the front seat. *And I really love the idea of fifty miles to the gallon.* Now, with both of her boys—Bruno had reached the status of one of hers—in high school sports, she was driving a lot. It certainly made it less painful, knowing it didn't cost her an arm and a leg for gas. *Next year, Eric will be driving!* She didn't want to think about that quite yet, so she pushed it out of her mind.

Mitch stood at the foot of the stairs and shouted up to Pat. "Girl, what are you doing up there? Didn't you say Deb was picking you up to go meet with Sal? Are you going to his office, or is he coming to Ashland to grill you?"

As Pat barreled past him, he tried to kiss the top of her unruly hair and make a grab for her. "Oh, no, you don't!" she said, dancing away from his reach and trying to put in an earring at the same time. "Why didn't he ask you to come, too? I need you there."

Mitch wrapped his arms around her and kissed her cheek. "Face it, Wonder Woman, you'll always need me. But when it comes to murder ... well, I like to read about it in the paper. Here's Deb now. Your carriage awaits. Call me if you need me to bail you out."

Deb watched from the car as Pat and Mitch said good-bye. She wrinkled her forehead, thinking about what Marc would say about their getting involved in another investigation.

We're not getting involved, she thought, practicing her speech for later. *We're simply being good citizens. After all, we were at the scene.*

She honked the horn, surprised at her impatience. After all, she didn't have to be back until three o'clock to see the boys' game. She had to admit that her impatience had more to do with getting to Washburn and learning more about the death than anything else. She smiled at Pat as her friend tripped lightly down the front stairs and opened the car door. "Really," Deb greeted her, "you look ten years younger!"

"Make that fifteen, and I'll buy lunch," Pat responded with a smile as she put on her seatbelt. "Let's hit the road, Jack!"

Deb realized as she pulled away that Pat was as eager as she was.

"Before you came this morning, you won't believe who came by," Pat said.

"Who?" Deb asked.

"Ruth."

"Ruth? Ruth Epstein? Why did she come to you? I've known her a lot longer! Did she tell you something about the body? Come on … spill."

"Don't get your hopes up. You know Ruth. She isn't going to tell anything inappropriate. She talked to me first because Linda and Forrest asked her to."

"But why?"

"Because they are sometimes members of the church, that's why. And Linda wondered if, when the time comes, if I would help with some kind of service." Pat adjusted her seat.

"Linda and Forrest?" Deb exclaimed.

"That's right. Turns out the body was Mac. Can you believe it?"

"Wow! I guess that makes sense. But she didn't tell you anything else?"

"Nope, well … not much … but since it couldn't have been an accident, it's going to be a while before the body is released," Pat answered with a self-satisfied smile, pleased that she was the one with inside information for once.

As they continued to drive toward Washburn, Deb and Pat went over the events of the previous day once again. Deb had driven to Washburn so many times before that her car seemed to know the way on its own.

"I still think that no one could have gotten a big canvas roll into the barn without help. There had to have been more than one person involved," Pat suggested. "Do you think the body was there all winter, or do you think someone put him there recently?"

"Search me," Deb replied. "That's for Sal to figure out. It was cold and dry in there, so it could have been either way."

"What I get the creeps about is that it was right in the middle of all the rest of all that stuff ... almost like the person who put the body there *wanted* it to be found."

Having dissected every bit of the scene, Pat reached for a bottle of water.

"Wow, look at how green it's getting. It's going to be a beautiful summer. I can't wait to see a sunset on the lake again."

"Maybe this weekend. Can you guys go out? Marc is eager to take Bruno out for his first sailboat ride."

Pat glanced in her side mirror. "Oh, oh," she said. "Slow down."

Deb took her foot off the accelerator and grimaced as she looked in the rearview mirror. "How long has he been there?"

"Don't know. We've been so busy gabbing. But the good news is, he doesn't have his siren on."

The words were hardly out of Pat's mouth when she saw the police car's light flashing and heard the whine of the siren.

"How is Marc going to feel about another ticket?" Pat asked.

Deb swore and pulled over. "Do you think we could have outrun him?"

The police officer strolled up to the car and tipped his hat as Deb rolled down the window. They recognized him as the officer who was well known for giving out tickets. "Hello, ladies," he said. "Do you know what speed you were going? I've been behind you through Washburn." Without waiting for a reply, he continued, "Could you please give me your license and car registration?"

"Hello, officer," Deb said politely. "I'm an attorney from Ashland, so I know the drill." If she thought he might let her off with a warning, as one professional to another, one look at his stony face burst that bubble.

"Ahuh," he said, looking Deb straight in the eyes. "Just doing my job, ma'am."

Deb visibly bristled as she handed him her license. *Adding insult to injury*, thought Deb indignantly. *It's one thing to get a ticket but quite another to be called "ma'am." When did I become a "ma'am," anyway?* She tapped her fingers on the steering wheel. "Could you make it quick? We're in a hurry."

The officer and Pat just stared at her, and then as he turned away, Pat started to giggle.

"Good one, Deb," she said as the cop went back to his car to look up her registration. "Not only do you irritate the one officer who always gives everyone a ticket—no exceptions—but then you broadcast that we are going to speed on our way!" She laughed.

While the women waited impatiently for the officer to finish writing the ticket, Deb's imagination flashed to a scene in the courtroom.

The ticket-writing officer was dressed in uniform and seated in the witness box in front of the jury, microphone pulled close. Deb, dressed in a tailored kelly-green suit and heels, was glaring at him with a stony face across the defense table.

"Officer, can you explain to the ladies and gentlemen of the jury how it is that you failed to record in your filed report the critical facts that you testified to here today?" she asked in her gruffest voice.

His face reddening, the officer shot Deb an irritated look. "Look here, ma'am, I know the drill, and what you are trying to do. I'm a police officer for the Washburn Police Department. Are you implying that I would somehow break the law?" he sputtered.

"Just doing my job, sir," Deb replied, *brandishing a whip behind her back.*

"Earth to Deb. Where are you?" Pat's voice broke into Deb's thoughts.

"Sorry, I was just fantasizing," Deb replied.

"If you wrote those fantasies down, it would make a good book," Pat answered lightly.

One hundred twenty-nine dollars in the red later, they were on the road again.

"Well, at least we helped them with their speeding quota," Pat teased her friend.

Deb groaned. *What will Marcus say? Better not tell him until after a good meal.*

"Listen, as long as we're early, let's go through the drive-through at the North Coast Coffee Shop," Pat suggested. "Maybe if we come bearing gifts, they'll give us a little info."

Deb navigated the Prius through the drive-through of the coffee shop in Washburn. "Two regular coffees and two cappuccinos," she said into the intercom.

Ten minutes later, Deb pulled up to a ranch-style brick building.

"What are we doing here? Pat asked.

"The Sheriff's Department building isn't in Bayfield; it's here, and so is the jail," Deb explained.

"Convenient, if he wants to throw us in the hoosegow."

"Funny, Pat," Deb answered as she opened the door.

"Uh, Deb, do you think you should park in handicapped parking, especially after our recent run-in?" Pat asked, pointing to the sign in front of them.

"Oops," Deb said, closing her door and backing up again. "Let's park over here."

They didn't know whether it was because it was small town or they were getting a reputation, but as the women walked in, the receptionist took one look at them and yelled through the door, "Salvadore, they're here!" She looked at them curiously, pointed to some old wooden chairs, and then went back to her computer.

The two women waited, watching the minutes tick by on the large clock on the wall.

"This coffee is going to get cold if he doesn't get out here soon," Deb whispered loudly, as if it were the greatest sin in the world to let good coffee-shop coffee go cold.

The receptionist looked up from her typing and shouted once more, "Sal, they came bearing bribes!"

"Don't they even have an intercom system for you?" Pat asked sympathetically.

"Sure," she grinned, "but he never answers it. And besides, this way is more fun."

After a few more interminable minutes of waiting, Sal came out of his office, with LeSeur following behind him.

"Thanks," LeSeur said, taking one of the cups from Pat's outstretched hand.

"Are you here giving him grilling lessons?" Pat couldn't help asking LeSeur, trying to hide her nervousness with sarcasm.

"No, I brought him my extra set of thumb screws, just in case."

Pat stood up and held out the other cup to Sal. "It's done the way you like it."

"Not much for a bribe," he teased, reaching out for the cup. "And I can't fix the ticket, ladies. I just heard it on the scanner."

The receptionist giggled.

"Come on back," Sal said, gesturing with his cup down the hallway to a back room.

The two women were led to a windowless gray brick room. It was definitely not from a scene from their favorite crime drama, *CSI*. Those scenes always looked so modern and fashionable. There was an old desk, with a chair on wheels that looked like it was left over from a school principal's office, a couple of folding chairs, and then, incongruously, a flowered couch with matching chair against the wall. A pretty mountain scene hung on the wall.

"My wife just bought new living room furniture," Sal mumbled, seeing Pat's look. "She thought her old stuff might dress up my office a little."

That's right, Pat thought, *He's recently married to a local girl, who obviously is nesting*.

"Oh, I think it dresses it up all right," Pat said politely. Deb kicked her.

"So," Sal said, sitting back in the old chair, "Sit. You understand that you are here to give us testimony of the crime scene you witnessed. In no way do we need, nor are we asking for, your help in solving this investigation. My buddy here warned me about you two, so let's cut to the chase. What's with you? Do you just have to be involved with every single murder on the South Shore? Remind me."

"We were there, at the Tent, volunteering, remember?" Deb started.

"Yup, and so were several dozen other folks. And none of them, as far as I can tell, are poking around in this death."

Pat and Deb gave each other a sheepish look.

"Of course not, Sal," Pat said, giving him her most convincing pastor smile. "Chill out. You must know that we aren't trying to butt in, but we were there. You called us, remember?"

It didn't seem to work.

"Just help us out, girls," LeSeur said winningly. "This is Sal's first big case, so don't screw it up for him, okay?"

"We wouldn't dream of it," Deb said indignantly. "We're just here on your request, so if you don't want us ..." She got up, as if to leave.

"No, no, sit down. Don't get your knickers in a bunch." Sal took out his pen and poised it over his pad. "We're just laying down the ground rules, as it were. Now, let's just start at the point at which you rolled out the canvas and the hand fell out."

Pat gulped. "Could we have a refill on coffee?" she stalled. She suddenly wished she didn't have to relive that horrible scene.

"Statements first, then more coffee." Sal felt he knew how to get information out of these two women.

"Have you found out who the body is yet?" Pat persisted, not wanting the men to know that she knew his identity. "It might be easier to think of it as a person if we knew who it was."

"Just tell us what he was wearing," Deb begged.

Sal shook his head and looked at LeSeur.

LeSeur shrugged. "It won't hurt to tell them. It's probably already all over town. It's Mac."

"Mac? Really?" the two women echoed in a convincing tone.

"If we answer your questions, will you answer a few for us?" Pat bartered.

Sal's voice became firm again. "This is not a two-way street. I ask the questions, and you answer them."

"What? Is this sixth grade, and you boys get to keep the secrets from the girls?" Pat scoffed.

Deb shifted her foot as if to kick her again, but Pat was quicker this time at moving her leg away.

"No, it's a murder investigation, and you are not relatives."

"So it really is a murder, not an accident?" blurted out Deb.

Sal shook his head. "It's an open investigation." He slumped back in his chair. He looked less like a mean deputy sheriff and more like a teenager, up to bat in the ninth inning, with two outs and his team counting on him to hit a home run. "Like my old supervisor, here, said, this is my first real case. I've got the mayor and the board president of the Tent breathing down my neck. If we don't get this done, quick and right, a lot of people will be without the pay they earn from the Tent. That includes hotels, restaurants, musicians, and gift stores." He shook his head wearily.

Pat reached out a hand, as if to comfort him. "You know we're connected to the Big Top. Is there anything you can give us to pass on? Everyone who works at the Tent is also worried."

"Ladies, I appreciate the thought, I really do, but don't mother me. I know how to do my job." Sal's shoulders straightened. "At least, I think I do."

"Enough," said LeSeur, and he turned on the recorder. "This is May 22. Please state your name and the town you live in for the record."

"I'm Pastor Kerry, and I live ... well, mostly in Ashland." LeSeur raised his eyebrows, and she went on. "What I mean is, we have a house on Chapple Avenue in Ashland and an apartment in Bloomington, Minnesota. You see, my husband still works down there, and—"

"Fine, fine." LeSeur turned to Deb. "And you?"

Deb cleared her throat and then said, "I am Attorney Deb Linberg, and I live on Chapple Avenue in Ashland also."

"And can you tell me why you were at the Tent on May 20?"

"Well, to volunteer, of course," Pat answered eagerly. "We were helping put up the Tent. Actually, I was supposed to just bring food, and Deb even baked a lovely coffee cake, but with the weather, not many volunteers showed up, so—"

"Okay, okay. Just try to answer in short sentences," LeSeur said in frustration. *This is going to take a while*, he thought, *and I'll need three aspirins for sure.* Turning to Deb, he asked, "And just why were you in the out building when the body was found? Short sentences, please."

When Sal stood up an hour later, he looked as tired as Pat felt.

How many ways could he ask the same questions? she wondered.

"Look, I know you two, all right?" Sal said. "And there might be more going on than you think. I know … I know that you think maybe you should help out, but if you start sticking in your noses, they just might get cut off. This is a poor county that can't afford to assign someone to watch you." He sighed, and then added, "Please."

Pat turned to Deb and nodded slightly.

Deb took up the lead. "I've known Forrest since he was a little kid. Linda and I have been friends since Forrest and my daughter, Julia, went to pre-school together. You knew that, right?"

"Nope," Sal replied.

"Well, we have been, and I am sure that this just tears Forrest apart. And don't even get me started on the money lost if the Tent has to start canceling shows. We get that you're in charge. It's just hard for us *not* to want to help."

Sal put his hands on his hips, his face hardening. "So you two are going to tell Linda you will solve this thing when you aren't busy running a church and a law practice? What next? Save the cheerleader; save the world?"

Uh-oh, Pat thought, looking to LeSeur for help. *He*

shouldn't be getting Deb's back up.

"Listen, buster," Deb said, quietly seething. "After a day spent with divorcing couples, parents fighting over children's rights, and calls from grandmothers who read me the riot act about seeing those same kids, solving a little death by unknown blunt object is like a tea party. And besides, Linda is my friend."

Pat and LeSeur moved in between the two.

"Hold on here," LeSeur said, putting his hand on Sal's shoulder. "No need to get riled."

Pat tried to move Deb toward the door. "We're not trying to get in your way, Sal," Pat broke in. "To answer your inkling, Ruth Epstein, the coroner asked me to help the family. They'd asked her to contact me. This has hit them pretty hard. We're not trying to get in your way. Right, Deb?"

"You knew all along?" Sal asked. "And you've been stringing us on all this time?

Deb blushed and nodded.

Dear Lord, Pat prayed silently, *just let us get out of here without a ticket for obstructing justice, if there is such a thing. Marc is never going to understand two tickets in one day!*

"I do think that's enough for the day," LeSeur said. He called out to the secretary, "Suzie, can you show these two ladies out?"

Later, as the women drove home to Ashland, Pat said with obvious fatigue, "I just can't believe how many times we went over that scene. It's really laser-burned into my memory banks now." She stretched out her legs, wiggling her toes. "At least they didn't separate us to ask us questions, like in the cop shows. I wonder why not?" She raised her arms above her head as far as the car roof would allow. Her shoulders and neck felt like steel. *Might have to go and get a massage from Holly. Having a masseuse in the church building might seem unconventional, but it sure is convenient.* "Hey, do you want to go into Bayfield to Gruenkes and have fish livers?" Pat asked, teasing her friend. Deb had never acquired a taste for any kind of livers, fish or otherwise.

"Probably because LeSeur was on the scene, too," Deb answered dryly, ignoring her friend's plea for eating out. "And all the other folks had stomped around the scene. How many clues can you get from mud?"

"You were pretty tricky, asking about the clothing," Pat said admiringly. "Was that to help date the season?"

"Oh, you know," Deb said, carefully glancing at her speedometer. *No use giving that cop another chance at me today.* "I think it was the shirt. It's pretty distinctive to the Monty and the Canadian Fiddlers band.

"But why Mac? After all, there are four other band members."

"Because he's the one connected here. It would make sense. It was a long time ago, but ever since Forrest was born, Mac's come around when he can to see his son. He fit it in, at least a few times a year, with his travels with the band. By the way, Forrest is a cute kid, isn't he? And so nice too." She shrugged her shoulders, getting back on track. "Truth is, it was just a good guess."

"I guess it was just hard to imagine that someone could be missing for months and not be missed. Odd how that it could happen," Pat mused.

"The band probably thought he was off with a lady for the winter or in detox. Linda and Forrest were used to his wandering ways, too. And I suppose they could have wondered if he was hiding out from Revenue Canada."

"Anyway," Pat said after a moment, "it's rather sad that a person could be gone months and not be missed."

"Never happen to us," Deb said reaching over and patting her friend's knee. "You and I can't even be gone an hour before someone starts looking for us!"

As if on cue, the phone started to sing. They both laughed, and as Deb answered it, Pat noticed a familiar police car hidden alongside the road in the trees. She rolled down her window and waved at the policeman, who scowled at her—and then turned a deep shade of pink.

Later that afternoon, back at church, Pat spread her sermon notes out on the desk in front of her and moaned, "Dear God, what am I supposed to do with *this* passage? And I'm not being rhetorical here. If you want me, a divorced person, to preach on a passage like this, you better send me something right now." Pacing to let off energy, she read the passage aloud:

A man who divorces his wife and marries another woman commits adultery against his wife. In the same way, a woman who divorces her husband and marries another man commits adultery.

"Please," she said once more, "I promise to be good. Send me a sign—lightning, anything!"

"Hi," said Esther, the church nurse, peeking in the door. "Do you need something, or are you just ranting indiscriminately? You don't have the poor janitor in here, giving him what for, do you?"

"Oh, hi, Es. No, the janitor is safe for now. What I need is a new text for Sunday. Any chance we can just rewrite it? Think anyone would notice?"

Esther laughed. "Change the Bible? Oh, they would notice, all right. Come on; take a break. Wendy and I are taking one. I brought some homemade cookies."

"Get thee behind me, Satan," Pat groaned. Then reconsidering, she threw her pad and pencil on her desk. "Sounds good. Maybe a break will help."

In the break room, Wendy dipped her cookie into her coffee, and said, "Have you looked at the second lesson yet? It seems that one is about loving and caring. Couldn't you go with that one?"

Pat smiled and gave her a hug. "You bet I could. Thanks."

As the tension settled, Wendy continued. "I heard you were there when they found the body at the Tent. Is that true?"

"Yup. It was weird. One minute, Deb and I were pulling out canvases from a pile, and the next, there was a hand sticking out from a roll. To tell you the truth, for a moment I thought Mitch and Marc were playing a trick on us. You know how they are."

"Gross. What did you do?"

"Not much. LeSeur was there, helping for the day, and so he took charge."

"Isn't that Sal's territory?"

"Sure, but he wasn't there, and LeSeur was. Frankly, I think he was glad of it. Sal's still pretty new to the job."

Esther took a sip and looked up. "Was it really Mac? I always loved his fiddle playing. And so did my Jim." She looked dreamily out the window.

"It was."

"And it's true that the body … that he was there all winter?" Wendy asked.

"Really too soon to tell. But it seems likely. After all, he was inside one of the canvasses."

"But how could that be? Didn't anyone miss him? No one called the police to report him missing?"

"I guess not. Sad, isn't it, that no one missed him after such a long time?"

"Well, it's just a shame," Esther agreed. "How does a person end up like that? I'm going to put him into the prayers on Sunday. He should be remembered. You know, I met him a couple of times. He was a charmer, that one. A great musician, but of course, not such a great father. You know about that, don't you?"

Both women nodded.

"But Forrest loved his dad, and Mac seemed to love Forrest back. How can a person be so disconnected that no one knows he died for five months?" she asked again.

To that, the other women had no answer.

As Pat walked home alone after work, her mind was filled with the latest Janet Evanovich novel being fed through her ear buds. She was jostled from her story as she felt someone bump into her.

"Hey! Watch where you're going, will ya?"

"Oh, sorry," Pat said automatically, puffing a little and pulling out her ear buds. She looked into the familiar face of Sam West, the photographer from the Big Top.

"Just kidding," Sam said. "You looked so serious, I just had to bump into you. How is the case going?"

"Why does everyone think I'm working on the death at the Tent?"

He laughed. "If you aren't, then how do you know which case I'm talking about? Get too famous, and I'll have to be your paparazzi." He lifted up his camera and pretended to click.

Pat laughed, too, and they walked companionably for a minute.

"No, really," Sam persisted. "Have you heard anything? After I got dressed out by the police for taking a few photos, I'm afraid to show any interest at all. Did they figure out what killed him?"

"I'm really not supposed to talk about it. Not that I know much, just that it was a blunt instrument. Why? Do you have any ideas?"

"No, but I've known Linda since ... well, since the beginning. And I worry about her and Forrest. Frankly, I never liked the way he treated her."

Pat stopped and looked at him. "That's right! You've been around since the Tent started. I've been racking my brain, trying to figure out what the blunt instrument is."

Sam looked at her, shrugged, and started walking again. "Could have been anything. There are lots of tools in that barn. A hammer ... crowbar, maybe? Heck, anything with heft would do." He held up his hand. "Even this might work."

Pat looked at the camera tripod in Sam's hand and a shiver went down her spine as she realized they were on the path with no one in sight. No one to call to if ...

"Hey, don't let your imagination run wild," Sam said, seeing her look of fear. "Sure, I had a thing for Linda. But that was a long time ago. I didn't hate the guy. I just thought he never grew up. Me, I wouldn't ever risk ruining my equipment on someone's head." With that, he jogged ahead, leaving her behind.

That's the trouble with murder in a small town, Pat thought. *Even when you finally find out who did it, you still have to live with the way you looked at others and thought, "Was it him?"*

Chapter Nine

The next day, Pat got into her Volvo, turned the key—and immediately felt guilty for driving. *It isn't because I'm falling into my old habits*, she told herself. *I'm late and can't walk to meet Deb.* She glanced down at the cookies on the passenger seat as she buckled her seat belt. *And a cookie is definitely okay once in a while,* she thought defiantly.

Just as she backed out of the garage, her phone rang. She quickly stepped on the brake and scrambled for her purse to catch the call before it went to voice mail. *Maybe it's Deb,* she thought. "Hello," she said distractedly, trying to stuff all the items back into her purse that had fallen on the floor.

"Hi, is this the pastor with a bent for murder?" inquired a deep male voice.

Her face flushed. Ever since they had solved their first murder, people had razzed her unmercifully. "Listen, smart aleck," she blurted out. Then she paused. She knew that voice. *Peter Thomas!* "And is this the army's June calendar star? How *did* you get that badge to stick on?" The hearty laugh on the other end of the line made her smile as she checked that the car was in park. *I don't need to roll into the street and hit a car when I'm on the phone with army intelligence!* "But I suppose if you had such a calendar, you'd all have to wear masks so no one could identify you."

Peter laughed again. "Don't even go there," he warned amiably. "I'm getting to the age that the photo would have to be taken in the dark or in a blizzard. Mine would have to be called 'undercover agent.'"

Pat laughed with him. They both were of a certain age, but Peter was amazingly fit. "So what's up?" Pat asked. "Do you need help with another case? Deb and I are available."

"Yeah, like that would happen. Actually, I'm giving you a call because I know about the Big Top case."

"Peter, I'm amazed!" Pat said. "How did you hear about that?"

"Well, LeSeur and I have stayed friends since solving the case in Ashland together last year. Even managed to go fishing a few times in the big lake when I've been in the state."

"And you didn't call for coffee?" she teased.

"Next time, for sure, Pat. I don't want to make that handsome husband of yours jealous, you know. But here's the thing: I know that you and Deb are looking into Mac's death. Don't deny it; save your breath," he said as she started to sputter. "Just thought you might like to know that the CIA and army intelligence ..." He paused. "Remember the young kid I brought up there? Andy Ross? Well, he's turning out all right. He and I were working together and looking into Mac's taxes and the possibility of his smuggling over the border. Not enough was found to prosecute, you understand, but still ... I'm calling to warn you because if drug running was involved, it could get dangerous."

"Oh, I don't think ..." Pat started but then stopped. *The band did go in and out of the country. I hate to think it, but what did I really know about Mac, except that he was charming and played a great fiddle?*

Just then, Pat's new iPhone beeped; it was Deb. "Thanks for the heads-up, Peter, but I've gotta go. I have another call, and I'm late to meet Deb already."

"Just let me know if you get in trouble," he said. "And say hi to Deb for me."

Pat walked up to the front window of the Black Cat and peered inside. She didn't see Deb, so she crossed the street to the bakery to get sourdough for supper and maybe a muffin.

"Sneaking into the bakery for a treat, Pat? Does your weight-watching friend know?"

Pat looked behind her to see who had spoken. "Oh, hi, Linda," she said, giving her a hug. "Don't tell, okay?"

"There seem to be more than enough secrets being kept in these parts today," Linda said, "so what's one more?"

"I'm so sorry for your loss and Forrest's. If there's anything I can do ..."

"It's going all right, I guess," Linda said with a sigh. "Sal's going to try to let us continue the shows, so that's good. Forrest is a little crazy. Who wouldn't be? He had a fight with one of his friends the other night. I just hope they figure this all out soon. It's hard, you know?"

Pat squeezed Linda's arm sympathetically. "Things will get better. Just ride the wave."

"Yup, I keep telling myself that. Pray for us, will you? By the way, I have that poached fish recipe and story you wanted for the church cookbook, but I didn't bring it into town with me. Sorry."

"It's okay. I'll pick it up. You've had more on your mind than fish recipes."

"Yes," Linda agreed. "If only I could be sure—"

Just then the beautiful woman behind the counter piped up, "Pastor Pat, halloo! What can I do for you?"

"Sourdough, please. Large." *Now what did Linda start to say?* Pat wondered. She paid for the bread and then turned back to Linda, but she was gone.

Deb sipped a freshly poured cup of French Roast as she waited expectantly for Pat at the Black Cat. It was eight in the morning, and Deb was tired from having overtaxed her brain the night before. There was so much to process all at once. The whole thing seemed just too incredible—an unexplained death at her beloved Big Top.

As she waited, Sarah Martin, the local town decorator and Deb's neighbor, approached her table and sat down.

"Hey, Deb, I heard that you and Pat were there when they found the body at the ski hill. That must have been a shocker!"

"You're not kidding," Deb answered. "This is one of the worst things that has happened in the Chequamegon Bay area in the twelve years since Marc and I moved here. And I am so glad I am not on the Chautauqua board right now," Deb said, rolling her eyes.

Sarah's eyebrows shot up in surprise. "You mean you're not president?"

"Nope. Eight years on the board of directors was long enough for me. And nearly three years as board president was *more* than enough."

"How did they rope you into that, anyway?"

"As a matter of fact, it was *your* mother who did it!" Deb replied. "Shortly after moving to Ashland, I got the standard invitation issued to all newcomers: 'You have to come to the Tent. It's the most unique musical experience you will ever have.' So Marc and I went to our first house show and were blown away. It was 'Riding the Wind.' After that, we went to all the others.

"Since that first show I have spent many sweet summer nights on that ski hill, with only the bright blue canvas cover between me and the stars—ecstasy! All those musical artists," Deb rhapsodized, "really expanded my horizons, like the gentle gilding of a brilliant sunrise in the morning sky."

"That tent is a hidden treasure, no doubt about it," Sarah agreed.

"Did you live here when it all got started?" Deb asked.

"I sure did! I remember when Warren and his buddies moved to the area. We were all young back then. That was a long time ago, and a lot of water has gone over the damn since." And with that, Sarah said her good-byes, and with coffee in hand, she pirouetted around and was out the door.

Sarah had no sooner left than Deb's cell phone began buzzing. Deb hurriedly dug into her jeans pocket to grab the phone. "Hello, Deb speaking," she sang cheerily. In response, she heard the deep, velvety voice of Carl Carlson. Carl was a big bear of a local radio announcer, with a quick, wry wit, and a heart of gold. He had taken over as president of the board after Deb had stepped down.

"Hey, Deb. Glad I caught you before you got to work. Is this a good time to talk?"

Deb detected an unusual urgency to Carl's usually unflappable voice.

"Yeah," she said, agreeing even though she was sure that this call would not be a short one. Carl rarely called her but when he did, it was usually to discuss Tent politics or to use her as a sounding board over the latest power struggle between the board and staff. And Carl just loved to talk.

"Have you heard the latest, Deb?" he asked.

"You mean, about the body?" Deb replied.

"Not that. You should have been at the last board meeting. You won't believe what happened! A group of board members are proposing to put up a bronze monument to the house band at the bottom of the ski hill, right at the entrance to Chautauqua. Problem is, the artist can only put in five people. How do we choose, after we put in Warren and Betty? So another faction says, 'That's going just a bit too far.' After all, they said, Big Top is so much more than just a few people. Why, there have been lots of local performers who have come and gone over the years that have also been part of the glue holding it all together. How could we possibly leave them out? Sure, they said. Warren's the one with the original idea, and his and Betty's genius created the house shows, but so many others put in their sweat equity, night after night. And on and on it went."

Deb listened intently, trying hard not to prepare her answer in her head before he was finished. She knew that Carl was going to ask her opinion in her role as former president of the board.

"Don't you miss dealing with this stuff?" Carl asked sardonically.

"The short answer is no. But you know, Carl, I never really cared that much about the nitty-gritty political battles that went on over the years. I always saw myself as a peacemaker," Deb replied.

"It was a quality that served you well, Deb. Especially during that high-conflict time in board and staff relations a few years ago. Do you remember that? I don't know how you survived being president then. Don't know how you did it."

"I guess I am just temperamentally unsuited to take sides between people I love. Reminds me too much of childhood struggles with my parents. I'm good at seeing the pros of both positions. Guess that's why I like to mediate those divorces," Deb responded.

"And here I am, about to ask you into the middle of yet another controversy," Carl said a bit tentatively.

Deb breathed in, asking the universe for guidance before answering. "A bronze statue? Well, Carl, that sounds hard. Maybe there's some middle ground, like putting a plaque in the front of the office or something," she ventured. *What next?* Deb thought. *Is this the Disneyland of the North? Next they'll be putting up plastic loons and neon hunters.*

Carl hesitated briefly after hearing Deb's answer, and then he pivoted to the real reason for his call. "Deb, I would be really remiss if I didn't ask you about what you think about this dead body that was found. I'm losing sleep over it, believe me. I could use some help on this. This is potentially disastrous. More disastrous, by far, than anything else that has happened in the past twenty-three years of this organization."

"Well, to be honest, Carl, I am still a bit stunned by the whole thing myself," Deb responded. *A bit stunned?* she thought. *Now there's an understatement! I am still freaked out by having come upon a dead body on my beloved Chautauqua grounds—and Monty McIntyre no less!* "And I share your concern over the PR problem with this and how it can be presented to the public in any kind of flattering way. It's a tough one," she commiserated.

"I just think that this thing has the potential to bring the whole thing down—whoosh—just like that. Imagine—no more Chautauqua on the hill during those sweet summer nights."

Deb shuddered at the thought. To her, the day Chautauqua went out of business would truly be—to borrow from the lyrics of "American Pie"—the day the music died.

"I'm really calling you today, Deb, because I need your help, and you're just the person—I mean, you and your good friend, Pat are just the ones to really look into this thing and help me put the best face on a miserable situation. You two have it all: you're both trusted members of the community, you have a demonstrated commitment to Chautauqua, and you're smart."

Resist. Resist! Deb thought as Carl continued his campaign spiel. She knew that he was trying to stroke her ego and deep down, she knew that there was no place for ego in this situation. Besides, she had enough going on in her life right now.

No! No! No! the voice in her head screamed. *You don't need this. Hang up now!*

But she didn't hang up. She heard the desperate plea in Carl's voice, and all she could think about was the awful prospect of Big Top being destroyed. It was a thought she just couldn't dismiss. No, she had to do what she could to keep that from happening, even if it meant more headaches or dealing with the teasing from Marc about once again trying to save the world.

"So, Carl, what is it exactly that you are asking us to do?" Deb replied gamely, in as confident a voice as she could muster.

"I want the two of you to try to find out what happened to poor Mac; to do an internal investigation, if you will, and report to me about what you find. That way, we can be prepared as a board to be proactive in our publicity, rather than waiting for this to trickle out in the media."

"I'll talk to Pat and see what she says," Deb agreed with a sigh. *After all, we would be less expensive than a five-hundred-dollar-a-day private investigator. Then again, if he hires a private detective, then everyone will know that he is snooping.* But in her heart, she knew exactly what her mystery-loving friend would say.

Chapter Ten

"Hi, y'all!" Pat greeted the crowd. Over the last two years, Pat had come to know the townies that came to the Black Cat. There was Wayne, the science and computer whiz, and Carol, whose photography business had started to get almost as successful as the sawmill owned by her lumberjack husband. And today, engaged in an intense debate with one of the new Northland College students, was poet and resident hothead, Rick. Looking around, Pat saw Deb sitting with Joel, the professor of music at Northland.

Pat smiled at her friend. "Let me just get my cup of java, and I'll be right there." Pat felt she was "glowing"—her word for when sweat went down her back—so she took off her sweatshirt, revealing a tank top. "Whew, I'm hot! Working out sure revs up my engine. I could eat three of those luscious, just-from-the-bakery cinnamon rolls," she said to Matt, one of her favorite baristas. After looking over her shoulder at Deb's watchful gaze, she stuck out her tongue.

"But I won't."

She slid her dollar and a quarter across to Matt and grabbed the cup he offered. "What's my horoscope today, Matt?" she asked, looking at the cup. The regulars at the Black Cat didn't get their daily astrology fix from the newspaper. They had decided long ago that the cups they were given would tell them something about their day. The collection of coffee cups at the Black Cat numbered a hundred or so, each with a different saying on it. And the baristas took their status as tellers of the future very seriously—the tips were better then.

"Yours has flowers today," Matt said sagely, "for 'everything's coming up roses.'"

"Thanks, buddy." As Pat debated which coffee to pick from the urns, she realized that the flowers on her coffee cup weren't roses at all; they were daisies. And the phrase that came to mind as she chose Mountain Blend was not "everything's coming up roses" but "pushing up daisies." That really wasn't the same at all, considering that the corpse they had found would soon be doing just that.

Just as Pat got to the table, Joel stood up. "See you, ladies. It's off to work for me. Actually, I love teaching these summer sessions."

"What are you teaching this summer?" Deb asked. She had thought about taking a class for fun.

"Oh, the history of jazz. And private lessons, of course. But summer is slower, so it gives me a chance to sit on the porch and play my banjo."

Pat smiled at the thought of hot summer nights and hearing the wonderful banjo sounds coming down the street. "We'll have to get together to do a little music," she called after him as he headed to the door. "See you tomorrow." Turning to Deb, she asked, "So, what's on the agenda for today?"

"Let's move to the booth in the back, and I'll tell you," Deb replied. As Pat slid into her seat with her daisy-covered mug, Deb smiled and raised her cup in silent salute, her face lit up with the excitement of new adventure and discovery. "Just a lot of sleuthing, maybe!" Deb squealed. "You won't believe the phone call I just had. Do you remember meeting Carl Carlson, the Big Top prez? The big guy with the white beard? He just called me! And he wants our help to 'monitor' the investigation into Mac's death."

Pat shot Deb a stern look. "Wait a minute, Deb! I have to stop you right there. We can't go inserting ourselves into a situation where we have no business—that's just asking for trouble. I don't care how much you want to please your Big Top buddies. *Boundaries*, remember?" Although Pat hoped her look had indicated "Don't argue with me; I mean business on this one," as she sat back in her seat, she thought, *But yes, of course we'll do it.*

"Come on, Pat, don't jump to conclusions. Just hear me out, okay?" Deb pleaded patiently. "First of all, I don't want more headaches in my life any more than you do. Heaven knows I have enough on my hands just navigating my way through an all-male household every day.

"But Carl is very worried that this whole thing could mean the end of the Tent. Imagine—no more Lake Superior Big Top Chautauqua on the hill. No more music. Just fold up the canvas and put it away forever and just let it molder in the barn," Deb went on morosely.

"As long as there's no body inside, you mean?" Pat joked lightheartedly, breaking the tension between them.

"Eeew, Pat, getting a little dramatic, aren't you?" Deb replied with a smile.

"Okay, so Carl is worried. What does he possibly think we can do to help, anyway?"

"He needs us to be the eyes and ears into Sal's investigation; to just keep him posted on whatever we can learn about where the investigation is going, so that we can help him manage the PR response by the board. It's all about schmoozing the public with these non-profits, you know. He didn't say anything about interfering in any way or about our doing any investigating ourselves." Deb's words seemed to fly out of her mouth now as she assumed her most per-suasive posture, honed over many years of practice in the courtroom. "This is really *big*," Deb said dramatically. "He is only asking us because he thinks we are *so* trustworthy."

"More like stupid!" Pat retorted.

"So, let's try to imagine whom we would consider as suspects if we were the ones investigating, even though we're not," Deb ventured, trying to move forward.

Pat, not for the first time realizing that she would have to play along, sat back and reflected. "Well, in old mys-tery stories I've read, the people closest to the victim are always the primary suspects. So, if I were Sal, I would be looking at Mac's band members, son, and jilted lovers," Pat said authoritatively.

"Lovers?" Deb asked, her voice perking up with inter-est at the thought of it. "I don't know anything about jilted lovers, except for Linda Johnson."

"Yeah, I wonder why she never married Mac."

Deb shrugged. "I suppose she didn't want to join Mac on the road or live in Cape Breton in the off-season—that's where the Canadian Fiddlers are based. Mac wasn't par-ticularly happy to be a father, but did what he could to be supportive of Linda's decision to keep the baby. She told me once that being on the road was no way to raise a child with roots and a sense of place. And besides, Linda loves the North Woods; she's an earth mother. I heard that Mac paid his child support and came to visit when he could." Deb took a sip of her coffee and shook her head. "I can't believe

Linda had anything to do with it. She's such a sweet woman. What motive would she possibly have to harm the father of her own child? Assuming, of course, that we're talking about an intentional act of malice. She doesn't seem to have an ounce of violence in her bones."

"Well, Deb, I won't waste my breath reminding you of all the so-called upright citizens I have met during all my years of ministry who have done despicable things!"

Deb nodded in agreement. "I'm going to play devil's advocate. Let's assume that Mac's death wasn't a murder. It *could* have been an accident."

"Death by blunt instrument. That's what the coroner said," Pat reminded her. "Let's just say, for example, that Mac didn't give Linda enough money, or that she was trying to protect her boy from something to do with his father that we don't know about. What if ..." Pat said, lowering her voice, "she was jealous of another woman?"

"Linda, jealous? After all these years?" Deb said incredulously. "No way. From what I've heard, her affair with Mac ended over twenty years ago. That just doesn't sound plausible. Besides, rumor has it that Mac had taken up with a hotty up in Herbster."

Pat held up her hand. "Just a sec. This deserves a second cup of coffee." She walked up to the counter. She pulled change from her pocket, but she didn't notice Matt's smirk in the direction of the new barista.

"So, will it be a body—I mean, a bagel—with your coffee today?" Matt asked.

"Wha-at?" Pat looked at him sternly. "Stop that! A person has died. I resent your implication that I like being involved in this." She pulled herself up in what she hoped was a haughty pose. "Besides, I have enough to do, working at the church right now."

Turning to the new guy, Matt said, "Nate, this is Pastor

Pat. You know, the one we told you about? Solved a murder right here at the Black Cat." He leaned over the counter and whispered conspiratorially, "So, really, who was it, and has Sal told you to butt out yet?"

Pat picked up her cup with as much dignity as she could muster. Then she broke into a grin. "Okay, so you've got me. And he didn't actually put it in those terms. It was more like, 'Do you want to go in one of my ugly cells for obstructing justice?'"

"See? What did I tell you?" Matt said as he nudged Nate. "Those two are at it again!"

Pat returned to the table, and Deb picked up where she'd left off, almost as if Pat hadn't stepped away. "In fact, I heard somewhere that it was the main reason he brought his band to town this year—the hotty in Herbster. Maybe it was just too much for Linda. Maybe this was the last straw!"

"Honestly, Deb, I don't think you're giving Linda enough credit. I think she's way stronger than that," Pat responded.

Deb looked out the window. "Okay, so you don't think Linda could have done it. What about Forrest, then?"

"Deb! Now you're really getting ridiculous. If I didn't know better, I'd think *you* were the one reading all those mystery books!"

"Hear me out, Pat—the pros and cons. Pros: Forrest is temperamentally suited to his sheltered life here in the North Woods, rubbing elbows with all sorts of musicians. Rumor has it, though, that Mac was deeply invested in the idea of Forrest's following in his footsteps as a fiddler. But once Forrest became a teenager, it got harder and harder for Mac to have influence over his son's musical tastes."

"Like every other parent in the world!" Pat exclaimed.

"Right. But call it guilt, call it projection, call it anything you want—Mac seemed compelled to step up his efforts to force his son on to a path that Forrest didn't want," Deb expounded. "Linda told me once that there were many arguments between father and son whenever he visited, and she got tired of the tension between them and began to step in. She couldn't stand Mac's onerous and condescending attitude toward her gentle, well-adjusted son—the son that she alone had brought up." Deb pursed her lips, her exasperation clear.

"All right then," Pat said. "Keep trying to convince me how Forrest could have been responsible. I'd love to follow your thinking into the wilderness, but honestly, here he is, a budding musician; he's well grounded"—she ticked off his attributes on her fingers—"he's well balanced ... a guy like that is going to just up and decide to off his pop one day? Makes no sense to me."

"You're such a skeptic, Pat," Deb sighed. "But from what I've learned in all my years of family-practice law, the chances are good that the kid had lots of abandonment issues, growing up without a father and all."

"There you go again, Deb. Injecting your own issues into someone else's drama," Pat challenged her. "Not everyone in this world has to be labeled with issues!"

"Well, let's just put aside the argument for now of whether or not Forrest felt abandoned by his father," Deb continued. "What if Forrest just blew a cork because of some argument between his parents? Say he was just trying to protect his mother. Maybe he found out about the babe up in the woods in Herbster and just didn't want his mother to have to endure one more insult."

Pat shook her head. "If you ask me, it's still a stretch for someone to do something so out-of-character and so serious, without a lot more reason."

Deb nodded in agreement and stared absently around the coffeehouse. She noticed a poster still on the wall that advertised Monty and the Canadian Fiddlers' appearance at the Tent from the previous season. She gestured with her head to Pat. "Do you think we should take it down?"

"Well, we certainly don't want Forrest or Linda coming in here and having more to be sad about, do we?" Pat assented.

Pat had barely gotten the words out of her mouth when the front door to the Black Cat opened and in walked a tall, bearded, distinguished-looking man wearing a jaunty black beret. The man glanced at the poster and then, visibly agitated, walked over to the wall and ripped it down.

Deb recognized him as Heinrich Wilson, the drummer in Mac's band. She gave Pat a quick kick under the table.

"Ouch!" said Pat, loudly enough for the whole room to hear. "Why'd you do that?"

Deb rolled her eyes toward Heinrich, then smiled and called out, "Hi, Heinrich! Hey, it's nice to see you out and about."

Heinrich paused for a moment. He took off his dark sunglasses and peered at the two women, trying hard to place them.

"I'm Deb Linberg. I met you at the cabin at the Tent a few years ago before your show. I was the board president for Big Top Chautauqua then. This is my friend, Pat."

Heinrich smiled tersely, looking slightly annoyed by the intrusion, but he extended his hand in polite greeting. "Nice to see you," he replied in a detached manner.

Seizing the opening, Pat said, "So sorry about your loss … Mac … I mean, it must be hard to lose someone so close to you. I understand that you had played together a long time. Mac was such a great guy. You must have been as shocked as we were about what happened to him. Do you know yet what happened?"

Heinrich narrowed his eyes as he studied Pat. "Thanks

for the sentiment, ma'am," he replied, "but the truth is, Mac wasn't always that good. Not to speak ill of the dead or anything, but I'm just being honest when I say that Mac was one of those performers who sucked all the oxygen out of the room for all the rest of the grunt workers around him. Not to mention all the money, publicity, and glory. He was an attention hog, that guy."

Deb's mouth dropped open in surprise. She was taken aback by his speaking so bluntly and unkindly about a dead crony. Quickly regaining her composure, she tried one of her professional calming techniques. "Well, I can see that you must have been hurt by Mac's behavior at times, but surely there were good times for you and Barry and Tim that you want to remember?" Deb asked hopefully.

"Sounds good in theory, ma'am, but you obviously never had the IRS coming after you for more taxes than a poor peon drummer can earn in a whole year!" Heinrich's eyes were flashing now as he turned abruptly to Matt behind the counter to order a large dark cup to go.

"So is that why you didn't miss Mac over the winter?" Deb persisted.

Heinrich laughed. "Hell, no. I just thought he was in rehab. Probably most people did."

"So much for commiserating with the bereaved," Deb said under her breath as she watched Heinrich head for the door. "A guy should never call me 'ma'am' twice. Let's put him on the list. What do you think about Heinrich, anyway? He's certainly mean enough!"

"Nah, I don't know if that's true," Pat responded. "Remind me: who are Barry and Tim?"

"Barry's the bass player and Tim plays lead guitar in Mac's band."

"That's right. As long as you're letting your imagination take flight, Deb, we might as well go all the way. Here's one you're not going to like. What about Sam West?"

Deb's mouth dropped open once again and she looked as though she'd been hit in the head with a brick. She sat quietly, apparently stunned into a pained silence. When she found her voice again, she said, "Sam? Really, Pat? Sam, the photographer? Of all people! I mean, Sam has his faults … heaven knows he's gotten into a few jams over the years. He's even thrown a few good temper tantrums, but Sam just doesn't seem to be the type to do something like this. Whatever makes you think he could?"

"Just suppose Sam was being blackmailed for some reason by Mac. Say that Mac had some dirt on him that threatened to destroy Sam's reputation."

"You mean he needed to protect his livelihood?" Deb asked.

"I mean he wanted to protect his relationship with a woman. Once again, I don't need to remind you that people are not always as they appear. Just the other day, I ran into Sam on the walking path, and he just gave me the creeps."

"What do you mean?"

"It was just a feeling I had," Pat answered. She shrugged and added, "Camera equipment is heavy, you know."

Deb pondered this thought for a time and then, glancing at the clock on her cell phone, she realized it was time to go to work.

Pat slumped in her seat, disappointed by their dead end. "I can see that we're certainly not going to solve this. And here we are again, analyzing and thinking that we know better than other people what the score is. To be continued …" she said with a smile.

"To be continued," Deb replied jauntily.

"One more thing, Deb, before you go. Do you remember Peter Thomas?"

"Peter from army intelligence? That Peter?"

"That one. He called me this morning."

"What did he want?"

"He called out of the blue to warn me. Said he kept a connection with LeSeur and had heard about Mac's death. Said something about Mac and the band *running drugs*."

"Wow. It sure is a small world. I want the full scoop on all of that, but right now I have to go save the world in court again. See you soon." After putting her cup in the dirty dish bin, Deb went out the door.

Chapter Eleven

Deb had barely closed the outside door to her law office before her secretary Kris's cheerful voice greeted her.

"Hi, Deb. Line one is Mr. Thompson. Line two is Ms. Thompson. They both want to talk to you right away."

Deb exchanged a knowing smile with Kris as she pondered how to respond. "Which one called first?" she asked.

"She did," Kris replied. "But he sounds more desperate."

Deb knew already that it wasn't going to be an easy morning. The Thompsons were divorcing, and she was appointed by the court to act as guardian ad litem, or legal advocate, for their eight-year-old daughter, Amanda. They were locked in a bitter tug of war over the child, a real struggle for power.

"Time to look for my magic wand again!" Deb said cheerfully. *Although it seems to be missing a lot lately.*

Deb knew that these parents expected her to work

miracles where no one else, not even themselves, could, especially if the miracle meant taking *their* side in the custody dispute.

"Kris, can you tell Ms. Thompson I'll get right back to her? Tell her I'm on another line, but don't tell who I'm talking to." Deb took a deep breath before picking up the phone to greet Mr. Thompson. "Hello, Jim," she said in her friendliest, calmest voice.

"Oh, Deb. So glad you are in today." Mr. Thompson sounded distraught. "You won't believe what *she* did last night. Honestly, I just don't recognize my wife anymore. She's changed into a totally different person—a witch—and it's scary. I just don't know what she'll do next."

Deb pulled out her yellow legal pad and pen and settled into her desk chair to hear him out. *The glamorous life of a family lawyer. This is why I get paid the big bucks*, she thought.

"And she wouldn't even let me come to my own house. Said I had to pick up my own daughter at Burger King. Do you know how humiliating that is for me?" he whined on. "Especially since she is the one who wants this divorce. And she went off to Florida on vacation with her mother last spring! Just who does she think she is, anyway?"

Probably a woman who needed a break from the whining, Deb thought. She looked down at her legal pad and admired the cartoon she had doodled. It was Mr. Thompson in a baby hat and diaper, whining and crying. Deb smiled.

After she listened to Jim's tale of woe, she focused on his upcoming court trial the following week. "Jim, I'm sorry that you're having such a hard time," she soothed. "It will get better; believe me. After you have a final court order, you'll both know what to expect. Meanwhile, what did you think about that settlement proposal I sent you last week?"

After calming Jim down and hanging up, Deb next

dialed Claire Thompson, Jim's soon-to-be ex-wife.

"Oh, Deb! You won't believe what happened last night! Jim was such a *jerk!* The nerve of him, thinking he could just come and pick up my daughter after school. I mean, even if he's always done it that way and even if she asked him to, that doesn't mean he should do it now. He should know that things just aren't going to be the same around here!" she ranted in a high-pitched voice. "Just who does he think he is?"

Probably just a dad who misses his daughter, Deb thought, feeling more like a baby-sitter than a professional.

"He's a menace; that's all there is to it! And my child is unsafe to be with him. He needs to be supervised at all times!" Blah, blah, blah. Ms. Thompson droned on, desperately trying to justify her contemptuous attitude toward her husband.

Deb's brain flashed to an image of the Thompsons as eight-year-old children .... *Each of them held a rubber club in their hands and stood in separate corners of an arena.*

Deb stood at the center between them, dressed in a tight neon-yellow T-shirt, short shorts, and a whistle in her mouth. Her taut, toned body glistened with sweat as she let out a loud blast on the whistle. As the parents relentlessly battled each other, Deb watched in wonder and tried to stay out of the way.

"Are you listening to me, Deb?" Claire asked.

Deb turned her attention to the task at hand. "By the way, Claire, what did you think about my settlement proposal?"

People get so angry with each other, Deb thought as her attention turned from the Thompsons to Mac and Linda. *I wonder how much would it take to kill someone you once loved?*

After Deb left, Pat sat at the Black Cat enjoying her second cup of coffee and waiting for her favorite parish nurse, Esther Marie, to show up. They always met Tuesday to catch up on parish news, and they realized early on that it was better to meet away from the church. Looking toward the door, she saw LeSeur stride in, talking to one of his young officers. Pat tried to will herself invisible and quickly looked down at the *Daily Press* in front of her on the table. "Don't let him see me," she silently called to the powers that be in her best Swami Ji imitation. Peeking over her paper, she saw LeSeur standing before her, arms crossed and feet planted firmly. *Guess I'll have to practice that one a bit*, she thought wryly. *This does not look good.*

"So, *Pastor* Pat," he said curtly, "I've just been having an interesting chat with Carl Carlson. You remember him? The board president for Big Top?"

"Of course I remember him," she snapped. "I may be older than you, but I am not in my dotage yet, and as I'm not your pastor, you can just call me Pat."

"Interesting thing," LeSeur continued, as if he hadn't heard her, "is not where he was or what he was doing but what he seemed to feel—that it was the consensus of the Big Top board that you and your busybody friend were 'investigating'—yes, that was his word exactly: investigating—this death. Of course I reassured him that we had talked and that you do not have a PI license. In fact, you could be arrested if you impeded this investigation." His voice had risen from its usual calm tone to one of stern authority.

Pat glanced at his sidekick, who was trying not to laugh at Pat's dressing down. "Wait just a minute," she replied, consciously keeping her voice down. "Since when do you accept secondhand information as truth?"

"Since Sal had Linda picked up for questioning this morning, and he's got reporters all over his jail. And a crew is searching her house right now."

"Oh, my gosh! Linda is in jail?" Pat jumped up. "I've got to call Deb. Where is that darn cell phone?" She reached frantically into her pocket.

"No," said LeSeur, pushing her back down in her seat. "You need to let Sal do his work. You need to take up quilting, or crochet, or even looking at porn on the Internet, for God's sake. Anything to keep you busy!"

She stared up at him, speechless, his hand still warningly on her shoulder.

"Hi, Pat ... Gary. Nice day, isn't it?" They both looked startled as Esther Marie stood smiling at them—although her sharp eye had taken in the hand on Pat's shoulder, and she felt the tension in the air. "Hey, Gary," she continued, as if she hadn't noticed anything amiss, "are you coaching Little League again this year?"

LeSeur took his hand off Pat's shoulder, like a small boy being caught by the teacher. "Yeah, I am."

Esther slid into a chair. "I remember when my husband was your coach. Do you remember? You were so cute, but you would get so mad, stomping your little feet when you struck out or missed the ball. Of course, you're not that little boy anymore, are you?" she said with a knowing smile. "You're a police detective now, for goodness sakes, and a good one, too."

He looked at her, and his face flushed. "Have a nice coffee, ladies," he said, looking at Pat. "Stick to burying folks, and I'll stick to how they got dead in the first place." He strode out, forgetting his coffee, with his junior officer trailing behind.

"Wow, looks like you're making more friends around

town," Esther joked.

Pat just shrugged and took another sip of her coffee.

Fifteen miles north, in the same gray rectangular room where Deb and Pat had been interrogated, Sal and Linda sat across from one another.

"Now you understand, Linda, that I just asked you in for routine questioning. I will be questioning everyone who might be involved with this death. By the way, I want you to know that I'm sorry for your loss." Sal cleared his throat. "But just to keep everything straight, I'm going to tape record our conversation. Is that all right with you? And also, I am bound to inform you that you have the right to remain silent and to have your attorney present, and that if you waive such rights, everything you say can be used against you in a court of law. Is that clear?"

"Sal, thank you, but this is not my loss. Mac and I were finished a long time ago. I'll help in any way I can but frankly, I don't know anything about his band or who he owed money to. I wasn't even there when they found him." She stretched out her feet in front of her. "Got any more of that coffee?"

The intercom buzzed on Sal's desk. He chose to ignore it, but it sounded again.

"Hey, boss! There are reporters out here!" Suzie said excitedly.

"Put them in the cooler," Sal answered. He got up and shut the door. "Coffee? Oh, sure, let me pour you a cup. It's with cream, isn't it? It's funny how many things people know about each other in a small town. Like your using cream in your coffee, and how Forrest is Mac's son." He handed her the coffee and noticed her face had reddened. "Now don't get all hot under the collar. That was a long time ago, and everyone knows you are a great mother. But I still have to ask you the questions. Are you ready?"

Linda took the cup from his hand. "Yeah, I know you're right. But this is so unreal. But if I was going to kill the bastard, don't you think I would have done it years ago, when it mattered?"

"Linda," Sal said sitting down across from her, "this is serious." Turning on the tape recorder, he said, "This is Tuesday, May 22, at 10:45. What is your name?"

"What is my name? You know my name." Seeing his exasperated face, she continued. "Linda Johnson."

"And what is your address?"

"Top of Ski Hill Road, Bayfield."

"And were you at the Tent on September first last year at Old Last Night?"

"Of course I was, Sal. You know that. You were there with your new wife."

"Just answer the question."

"Yes, I was, and so was half of Bayfield. Just ask me what you really want to know. Ask me if I killed him."

"Did you?"

"Are you *crazy*? He was a run-around bastard who couldn't keep his eyes off a pretty girl to save his soul. Lord, how many times I wished that he could have. But it just wasn't in him. So, did I want to just get him out of our lives sometimes? Yes, I did. But did I kill him? You just try to pin that one on me, Sal, and you'll be sorry."

"Settle down. So your answer is no? You didn't kill him?"

"Damn straight."

"So where was Forrest on that night? Was he with you?"

Suddenly, it got very quiet in the room. Linda folded her arms and closed her eyes. "I've changed my mind. I will not answer your stupid questions."

"Linda, are you refusing to answer my question?"

Linda opened her eyes, pressed her lips tightly together, and, standing up, threw her coffee on Sal's new white shirt. "I want to see my lawyer!" she said loudly.

The day had been a long one for Deb, so it was a relief to leave the office and pick up the boys from their tennis match in Bayfield. She loved the noisy boy-ness in her van. Turning her head, she called out, "Boys, I've got to stop to pick up a recipe for Pat. It'll just take a minute."

"Like you ever cook!" Eric smirked. Then he groaned. "Mom, we're starving."

"Like that's something new!" Deb retorted gaily. "I swear I'm buying enough groceries for the whole team."

"Growing boys, Mom, growing boys," Bruno sang out.

She loved hearing Bruno call her "Mom." She turned into Linda's driveway, turned off the ignition, and jumped out of the car. "Be back in a jif!" She threw the boys a bag of chips. "This will hold you over."

As she shut the door, Deb could hear Eric trying to explain to Bruno what she'd meant by "jif."

Linda opened the door, looking a little confused and a lot like she hadn't slept for days. "Oh, hi, Deb. Did I forget something?"

"No, no," Deb reassured her quickly, entering the cozy A-frame. The large open room was furnished sparsely in rustic pine. "I hope you don't mind that I stopped by. Pat said you had a recipe and story for the church cookbook, and I offered to get it. Is this a good time?"

Linda's tired face lightened. "Of course. The deadline is coming up, isn't it? Sit down, won't you?" She led Deb toward a large overstuffed lounger in the main room. "I'll just run upstairs and get it. It's all ready."

Deb sat by the stone fireplace. Her head hurt from trying to figure out what could have been used to kill Mac, not the least because it would be sort of fun to figure it out before the police or Pat did. Sighing, she shook her head and leaned back in the soft chair. *Face it, girl, it could have been anything. There are probably a million things in a house that could be used to hit someone over the head. We might never figure it out.*

Deb wondered what the police had looked for when they searched this house. She sighed again. *Good thing they didn't search our house*, she thought. *The way it looks lately, they might get lost in the mess and never be found again!*

Linda came quickly back into the room. "Thanks for picking this up. Would you like a cup of tea?"

"I would love it, but I have two voracious tennis players waiting in the van." Looking back at the fireplace she asked, "Have you been rearranging? It seems like things are different in here."

"No, the *police* were rearranging. They went through everything." Linda looked around the room, as if it belonged to a stranger. "It felt like being violated. It didn't help that Forrest came home in the middle of it and threw a royal fit. They were pretty good about it, though. At least they tried to put things back in order."

Do I dare ask? Deb wondered. She hesitated briefly, then said, "May I ask ... did they ... take anything with them?"

"Yes. Don't you see what is missing?" Linda said, pointing to the mantle. "They took my mother's antique candlesticks. Can you imagine?"

"Oh, my gosh," gulped Deb, "shades of Colonel Mustard in the library with the candlestick." Before she could say anything more, a loud "Mom-m-m!" came from outside the door. Deb smiled. "My boys. The natives are getting restless." She stood up and hugged Linda. "Thanks for the recipe and story," she said, and then as she turned to leave, she called out toward the door, "Coming! Keep your shirts on."

Chapter Twelve

That Thursday night, Deb put on her size-small Big Top fleecy sweatshirt and then called to the boys to get in the car. *Nice to be a small person once again,* she thought happily. *Marc really likes the new me.* After a quick stop at Pat's house to pick her up, they were on their way.

Deb was always excited for New First Night, the opening of the summer tent-show season at Chautauqua. She was especially eager to get to Bayfield on this particular night. It seemed a miracle that the show would even go on this year, what with Monty's death and all the distractions.

Deb expected that tonight would be especially fun. For one thing, it would be Bruno's first time attending a show at the Tent. And this would be one night, for a change, when she and Pat had no responsibilities. They were just going to watch a show as spectators and enjoy themselves.

"Mom, why do you always volunteer at the Tent?" Eric asked from the backseat.

"The show could not go on without volunteers," Deb replied good-naturedly. "Volunteers do everything at Big Top—all the nitty-gritty details of putting on a show. Everything from selling tickets to directing parking, ushering, and selling sweatshirts."

"What's nitty-gritty?" Bruno asked.

Deb glanced at Bruno in the rearview mirror and smiled. "I'll have to think about that one and tell you later."

"What do you like to do best?" Bruno asked.

"Oh, our specialty—mine and Pat's—is selling raffle tickets for the end-of-summer raffle. But that's for another night."

"Right," Pat agreed. "Tonight, we're just going to relax, let go of our worries, and just enjoy the show."

No thoughts of dead bodies, suspects, or that pesky Detective LeSeur, Deb thought. *None of that is strong enough to stand in the way of the magical musical experience under canvas.*

Deb pulled the Prius into the dirt parking lot at the foot of the ski hill. "Well, what's it going to be for you tonight, Pat? Fish boil or salad?" Deb teased, her mind going first to the subject of food.

"Fish boil?" Bruno asked incredulously. "I only eat red meat. What's this about a fish boil?"

"Oh, Bruno, you haven't truly become a part of this place until you experience a real northern Wisconsin fish boil. It's a Tent specialty every Friday night, all summer long," Pat instructed. "Imagine: potatoes, onions, and whitefish, boiled all together in one pot. M-m-m!"

"I prefer *chipa guazu* myself," Bruno said with a smile. "You'll have to come to Paraguay to try it. I'd just like to see you both find out for once what real food tastes like."

Deb smiled. Bruno managed to sound charming even when he was complaining about something.

They all got out of the car and walked to the food tent, drawn by the smell of grilled burgers. The food tent was lined on the right by a long red counter that held condiments. Behind the counter were the beer spouts, coolers with sodas, rows of candy, and the grill. To the left of the counter was a large sand pit filled with picnic tables, and farther to the left was a counter containing the Big Top gift shop, where sweatshirts and CDs could be purchased.

Deb and Pat ordered chicken salad and the local favorite brew, Leinenkugel's beer, which everyone referred to as "Leinie's." They sat down to eat at one of the picnic tables under the food tent, where the aroma of boiled fish permeated the air.

"M-m-m, this is great," Deb said to Pat. "There is just something to be said for eating outside."

"There is something to be said for someone else cooking!" Pat joked, taking a big bite of her salad.

"There's something to be said for being able to have something that's not chicken," Bruno said, smiling as he took a large bite of his hamburger.

"Yeah," Eric agreed. "Bruno can get the 'authentic northern Wisconsin experience' some other time."

"Race you up the hill later!" Deb teased to Pat, as she quickly finished her salad.

"Sorry, but you'll have to wait till next time," Pat replied. "I didn't wear my running shoes tonight."

Electricity was in the air, and Deb picked up on it as she looked around the crowd and recognized the faces of so many friends and neighbors. It was a large crowd, and everyone seemed excited to come together for the start of a new season. It was like a big family reunion. Nancy, the Lutheran pastor from Washburn, was selling raffle tickets. Nancy was glad-handing, back-patting, and hugging nearly everyone she saw.

Deb's ears perked up as she caught part of a conversation behind her. "Can you believe it was there the whole winter without being found? And they still don't know who did it."

"Yeah, the murderer could be here tonight," another voice piped in. "I heard the hand fell right off the arm; it was so rotten."

Pat was finishing up the last bites of her chicken salad. It suddenly didn't taste very good. *What is wrong with these people?* she thought. Carl approached their table with a big smile. He gave Deb a bear hug and then turned to Pat.

"So good to see you two," he said. "Thanks for coming. How about joining us in the Spirit Cottage before the show? The board is having a little reception for the band and staff before the show goes on to kick off the new season."

Deb felt honored to be asked to such an intimate gathering and quickly nodded her head in agreement. "Come on, Pat. This will be fun. Eric and Bruno will be fine on their own. Look—they're running up the ski hill to enjoy the view."

Something I'd never be caught dead doing, Pat thought.

As they entered the large screened-in porch of the crowded log cottage, Deb and Pat were immediately caught up in the celebratory atmosphere. They noticed a huge spread of tasty-looking appetizers and tantalizing desserts, prepared by the caterers at Good Tyme, a restaurant in nearby Washburn.

"Darn! Why did we bother to eat?" Deb asked, a hint of frustration in her voice.

"Just because it's there doesn't mean we have to eat it," Pat admonished her gently. "Besides, we didn't come for the food. We came for the people!"

Deb nodded, although she couldn't tell if Pat's new-found enthusiasm was genuine.

"Is it true that the body was so rotten they couldn't

identify it?" a voice whispered behind her.

"I heard that someone at the Big Top was behind it," whispered another.

Just then, Byron, one of the visiting musicians, walked briskly into the room and approached the tables with disdain, as if he were a cranky judge at a county fair. He eyed the beautiful food, which the crowd was "oohing" and "aahing" over, quickly did an about-face, and strutted to the door to the dressing room. "Where's Marcia?" he bellowed, oblivious to the crowd close beside him. "I was told that Marcia was the hostess tonight! Where is she? I want McDonald's! If I've told them once, I've told them a hundred times—I can't go on stage without my usual pre-performance favorite. None of that Gucci-rich stuff for me!" he said indignantly to no one in particular.

"Jerk!" Deb and Pat said almost at the same time, smirking at each other.

Deb did her best to savor being outside for the rest of that beautiful evening. The sound of a loud clanging bell signaled the five-minute warning and reminded them that it was time to take their seats in the big tent. Eager to see the new season begin, the crowd made a beeline to the entry of the Tent.

They didn't have long to wait before the house band broke into a rousing chorus of "Ballyhoo."

I can't believe another year's gone around,
Is that a Big Top Chautauqua lying on the ground?
Ballyhoo ... Ballyhoo ... Ballyhoo!

The crowd went crazy with wild applause. At the end of the song, Carl strolled up to the microphone at center stage and began the season in earnest.

"Ladies and gentlemen, welcome to another season

at the Big Top. Please give a grand Big Top welcome to Gerald DePerry, our resident Native American storyteller from neighboring Red Cliff. Gerry is from the Band of Lake Superior Chippewa, or Ojibwa tribe.

Gerry walked nobly to center stage, dressed in his full traditional native garb. He carried a large eagle feather in his right hand. In his left hand, he held a large staff, decorated with feathers. On his head was a chieftain headdress made of feathers. His leather tunic and leggings were beaded in patterns of turquoise and white.

Gerry smiled at the audience. "Thank you, Carl," he began. "It's always good to be invited here to share stories with you about my people, especially stories where the Indian isn't a thief."

The audience laughed.

"Many, many years ago, when Wenabojoo—our Anishinabe word for God—was familiar with this part of the country, his favorite spot was Lake Superior." With his quiet power, Gerry instantly had the audience's rapt attention. "And in his travels around the Bay, he noticed that a giant beaver made his home here. Wenabojoo decided to capture this great beaver, and he built a dam to keep him in this part of the bay. He used rocks, sticks, and sand and built his dam across the bay. Long Island still exists as part of the dam that Wenabojoo built.

"Poor Wenabojoo was disappointed because he didn't build his dam strong enough, and the giant beaver escaped and swam out into Lake Superior. Wenabojoo was so angry that he took handfuls of sand and threw them at the beaver as he swam away. As far as he could see, Wenabojoo kept throwing things, creating an island with each handful. And that is how the Apostle Islands were formed."

Gerry walked to the center of the stage, where a large wok-like bowl lay atop a tall stool. In the bowl was a bundle of sweet grass. "We usually don't tell stories like that until wintertime," Gerry said, "so this evening, I put out some tobacco and said a prayer, because I didn't want to offend any spirits that may be here tonight." Taking out a match, he lit the end of the bundle and then slowly and carefully walked down the steps from the stage and into the audience, carrying the bowl with him.

"Tonight, I have been asked to smudge the tent. Smudging is a traditional Native American purification ritual, done to drive away any evil spirits and create a physical space filled with harmony."

Deb inhaled deeply as the smell of sage and sweet grass permeated her senses. Gerry walked past her seat as he circled the inside of the tent, wafting the smoke with his eagle's feather. Deb turned so that the smoke could envelope her whole being.

Ah-h, let it be real, she thought, catching a twinkle in Pat's eye. Once again her friend seemed to read her mind, as she, too, twirled in the fresh scent.

"Is this the stuff that takes you to a higher plane," Pat joked, "or just gets you high?"

Deb looked at Pat, as she listened to the native drums and the hypnotic sound of Gerry's voice. "It's real in that I want this place cleansed of the evil that happened here," Deb said. "It's real in that the smudging does its job and makes a new beginning."

Pat put her hand on Deb's. "I know, but the truth is, it won't be gone until we find out who did this terrible thing. Can't you feel it?"

Deb nodded, a troubled look on her face. "Yes, I know you're right, but tonight let's just enjoy the opening of one of our favorite places. Deal? Tomorrow we'll carry on."

"Yes, let's," Pat agreed.

After the lively performance by the house band, Byron's set seemed to fall on its face. Even so, the night was relaxing. Deb arranged a ride home for Eric and Bruno with the Epsteins. She and Pat wanted to linger a bit longer in the new season of magic.

Deb walked into the T-Bar, aptly named to coordinate with the ski resort business that took over the Chautauqua grounds during the long winter season. Pat was seated with the house-band members in the corner. Phil, Jack, Ed, and Tom were sitting with Sam West and seemed involved in a post-mortem of their performance on stage. The band members sounded like a gaggle of excited geese.

"Hey, Deb," Phil called out to her. "Pull up a chair and come throw a few back with us." He gestured to an empty chair next to Sam.

Wow, this is a happy crowd, Deb thought, as she made her way through the crowded room to the corner. *They obviously feel as good about their performance as the audience.* Deb was surprised that after all the years of doing shows, these musicians still worried about whether or not they were good.

"Hi, guys," Deb said, nodding to the excited group. "Looks like the season is off to another great start. Can I buy you a round? Here's to you all. How do you keep doing this year after year?"

"It's the nature of show business," Tom responded with a happy smile.

Pat, as usual, the life of the party, lifted her glass to toast the band. "Here's to the music and here's to you!" she chimed enthusiastically.

"And lest we forget, here's to the one who no longer does his music," Deb added.

They clinked their beer mugs, and Deb reached down for her purse on the floor to get her wallet. As she did so, she noticed a small, folded piece of paper by Sam's feet. She assumed it was a napkin and picked it up, thinking absently about litterbugs. But after reaching for it, she realized it was a handwritten note. And as she read it, a chill ran down her spine.

The din from the crowd had grown increasingly loud, but Deb sat quietly, trying to decide what to do. Her brain was working overtime now, as she thought about what she had seen written on the piece of paper. She clutched it tightly in her hand, not wanting anyone else to see. She wanted to look at it again, just to be sure of what she'd seen, but she told herself, *No, it's none of your business. This is not your property!* Her lawyer and good-girl brain, the part of her that was trained to respect and protect the privacy of others, screamed at her to leave it alone.

But this is about Mac—a dead man! intoned the curious, inquisitive other voice in her head. After debating a few moments more, Deb's nosy brain won the day.

"I'll get the next round!" she announced, getting up and walking toward the bar. "Send a round over to the table in the corner, and add a Diet Coke for me, too," she called to the bartender. Then she walked to the ladies room and quickly entered one of the stalls. She reached into her purse and opened the paper once again.

Just one little peek, she thought. *It won't hurt anything. Yeah, just like opening Pandora's Box.*

> Sam –
>
> I know about the affair with Linda. We need to talk soon. Call me tomorrow or else I have no choice but to share your little secret with the others.
>
> Mac

Wow, Deb thought, taking a deep breath. She committed the words to memory, then washed her hands and joined the happy crowd. Just as Deb sat down at the table and her glass of Diet Coke, the group started to disband. As people got up to leave, she sat still as a stone, breathlessly trying to decide what to do with the crumpled note she held in her hand.

Sam looked at the note in Deb's hand. Without a word or so much as a facial tic to belie what he was thinking, he quickly snatched it from her and stuffed it into his front vest pocket.

"That's mine. I dropped it!" Sam said.

Deb looked into Sam's eyes for some clue as to the significance of the note. She saw no trace of guile or ire there. Instead, ever the smiling artist, Sam graciously shook her hand.

"Thanks for coming, Deb," he said. "It's always good to have so many faithful supporters like you and Pat here on New First Night."

Can't wait to tell Pat about this! Deb's thoughts were troubled as she turned and walked into the night air for the ride home.

Chapter Thirteen

"Do you want a cup of coffee? A pop?" the night nurse asked softly.

After arriving home from the show, Pat had been called to the hospital to sit with an elderly parishioner.

"No, thanks," Pat responded, looking up from the chair beside the bed with a smile.

Pat didn't mind these calls in the night. It reminded her of times she would get up with her children when they were small. After they were fed or changed, she would sit for a while, content to just hold them or rock them. *It's that twilight time*, she thought, *when the barrier between heaven and earth is thinnest. Quiet waiting time. Beginning and ending time.*

Taking the elderly woman's hand, Pat smiled. "Eleanor, can I get you something?"

"No, honey. I suppose I should call you 'Pastor,' but you're just like a friend to me." Patting Pat's hand she smiled a broad smile that shone no less for the lack of her bottom bridge. "I'm through wanting anything at all. But it surely is nice to have you here waiting with me."

"Waiting?"

"Oh, come on now, this is no time for pretending. I know I'm dying, and so do you. I've lived a long life. Some good and some not so good. My John's been gone for ten years now, and Josh, my boy, is living in Seattle and has given me three wonderful grandbabies. You know there is a time for everything. My best friend, Sadie, went two years ago. I swear I miss her every day. It's time." She paused a moment to catch her breath. "She'll be waiting for me, you know. Can you keep a secret?"

Pat nodded and leaned in to listen. "Oh I've been known to keep a few for special people like you."

"Well, last Sunday after church, I went home and had a nap on the couch, just like usual."

"Am I making my sermons too long for you?" Pat teased gently.

"No, dear, I'm just winding down. I'm like the grand old pocket watch that was my father's. No matter how well I kept it up, it finally stopped. You'll see that Joshua gets it, won't you? Anyway, about last Sunday. I was napping, and suddenly, right there before me was Sadie. Only she was young and strong, like when we first met. And I said, 'Sadie, what are you doing here?' I was a little afraid, to tell you the truth. After all, I knew she was dead. But she said, 'Why are you afraid of me after all these years? I came with a message. The truth is, I asked to come. I've so missed you these two years.'

"So I said, 'Are you here to take me up?' But no, she just sat right down beside me, asking me about the grandbabies and the neighbors, just like we used to do. Finally, she kissed me on my forehead and said, 'Here's the message, friend. It's almost time. Don't be afraid. I'll be waiting for you at the gate.'" Eleanor looked up at Pat. "So I expect she'll be waiting for me, with John by her side."

Pat leaned closer. "Do you really think there is a gate to heaven?" she asked.

The old woman chuckled. "I don't know. I don't even know if there is a heaven. But I do believe that there is something, and I'm thankful for all I had here. And whatever it is, those two will be waiting for me. Not logical, I suppose, but I just know. Still, it's a comfort having you here. And I thank you."

"Let me wipe your lips," Pat offered. "They look dry." Gently, Pat dabbed the old woman's lips with a damp sponge.

"Thank you kindly. That's what my mother always said. Now, can you do two favors for me?"

"Sure." Pat's heart beat a little faster. Last requests, she'd found, could be tricky.

"First, I want you to tell my son it's okay that he didn't get here to see me off. I know that he loves me, and I will love him forever. Okay?"

"Sure." Pat took a deep breath and wiped at the tears forming in her eyes.

"And next, I want you to sing that Jesus song at the funeral. Make sure Susie plays it on the piano, not on the organ. Nice and loud, do you hear?"

"Of course," Pat agreed.

"As a matter of fact, I'm feeling a little tired. Could you maybe sing it for me now? And I'll just rest a bit." She let out a long relaxing sigh.

Pat wondered what other people in the beds around them thought as she softly started to sing. "Jesus, Jesus Jesus, there's just something about that name ...." She hoped it would soothe their pain, whoever they were.

Her midwife job done and the woman delivered, Pat

drove home as the sun began to peek out in the east. Her thoughts drifted to Mac. *He didn't get to live his life to a ripe old age of ninety-two, or see his son marry, or bounce grand-babies on his knee. No one held his hand at the end times. I don't care what Salvadore says. If I can do anything to find his killer, I will. No one should have to die alone.*

Chapter Fourteen

He found himself once more sitting on the familiar wooden chair.

"Silly cops ... so far they haven't even figured out how he died."

He dragged a stick on the dirt floor and couldn't keep his eyes from that corner.

"Although I suppose it could have been anything handy."

Abruptly, he felt a chuckle gurgle up in his chest and burst out of his mouth. He was shocked at his own reaction in this place.

"In this place, of all places, get a grip," he told himself. "Who would have thought that it would be so easy to kill someone?"

He almost laughed again. Rocking the chair back and forth on its rear legs, he repeated his mantra:

"It's going to be okay ... okay."

Chapter Fifteen

"Only ten more minutes left this hour to meet our goal of seven new pledges! Get on the phone now and call 888-218-1212 to donate to Wisconsin Public Radio's spring fund drive."

Carl Carlson's rich bass voice woke Deb the next morning. She flailed her arm toward the radio next to her bed, saying with obvious irritation, "Quick, Marc! Turn that thing off! I can't stand to wake up to all that noise!" She rolled over and put the pillow over her head.

Marc turned off the radio and bounced out of bed, heading for the shower.

That was one great show last night, Deb thought. She relished savoring the experience of the night before as long as possible. She wanted the musical high to extend at least into the next day. The last thing she wanted was to start her day with Carl making her feel guilty about not donating enough money—as if she needed anything else to feel guilty about.

Even beneath the pillow, Deb was jarred into the day once again by the sound of the phone ringing.

Why isn't the maid getting that? Deb mused. *Right. I don't have one.* It was no use waiting for someone else to pick up. She could hear Marc in the shower, and she knew that a volcano could erupt in the house and Bruno and Eric wouldn't hear it. *I've got to train the dog to answer the phone.*

"Good morning," Deb said, mustering her most cheerful morning voice. She was surprised to hear Linda's strained, muffled voice on the other end.

"Deb? Did I wake you? I just really need to talk to you right away." She seemed to shudder and then continued in a torrent of words. "I don't know how much more of this I can take. There's a limit to how much one human being should have to endure. I desperately need your help ... I need an attorney."

Deb listened intently as she mentally ticked off all the work responsibilities that lay ahead of her in the day. She took a deep breath as she let go of the notion that she was in control of her life or even of this new day. *As if I ever am,* she thought. "Okay, Linda," Deb said soothingly, "you sound really upset. Can you meet me at the Black Cat this morning? Pat and I usually meet there every day. I don't know if I can help you, but I'll make time to listen."

"I'll be there in an hour!" Linda replied cheerfully, although the cheerfulness seemed forced.

"Great, see you soon," Deb answered. "Meantime, remember, Linda, things are never as bad as they seem." As Deb hung up the phone, a little voice in her head said, *Sometimes, they're worse!*

After a hot shower to boost her spirits, Deb sat down to breakfast with Marc and quickly discussed their plans for the day.

"Don't forget that I want to take *Hot Sauce* out on

the bay this afternoon for a maiden voyage," Marc said, His tone was one of unadulterated joy. "I took the afternoon off. You know I've been waiting all winter for this. It's time to get tuned up for the regatta in Lake Geneva in a few weeks."

If that boat was a woman, I'd have to be worried, thought Deb.

"Now that the Tent is up, there won't be many chances for me to get you out on the lake with me," Marc continued.

"True enough," Deb agreed.

Deb and Marc had learned the fine art of trade-offs that inevitably evolve between long-married couples. He raced his sailboat on weekends more than she liked, and she went to the Tent more often than he preferred, each of them conceding the passions of the other.

Just then, Bruno danced into the kitchen. "Yippee! I'm going sailing later. Dad's taking me out, too!"

Another man lost to the boat! Deb sighed.

By the time she emerged from her house for the five-minute walk to the coffeehouse, Deb was a renewed woman. *Maybe I'll just jog the four blocks.* Marc had already left for his twenty-five-mile commute to the medical clinic in Red Cliff. Eric and Bruno had headed to the tennis court for a leisurely match.

What is it about boys that they can go so easily and quickly from dead sleep to out the door without as much as a transition? It seems as natural to them as breathing, Deb thought. She inhaled deeply, trying her best to be aware of her surroundings. *What a gorgeous day!*

There was a fresh, cool crispness in the air that foretold an afternoon that would be sunny and bright. The morning bird chorus of cardinals was alive and well, singing a symphony. Deb noticed the tulips emerging from the small front-yard gardens and the buds popping from the trees on the boulevard as she walked down Chapple Avenue to the

Black Cat. She could smell the scent of the big-lake water, even though it was nearly half a mile away.

Pat, as usual, was already waiting as Deb walked contentedly into the coffeehouse. The usual gang was missing this morning—the big front table was empty.

Thank goodness, Deb thought. *I don't need to feel any more guilt about sitting with Pat and not joining the crowd. Heaven knows it's becoming harder and harder to have any private time to talk uninterruptedly without being joined by one of our coffee klatch friends. Today is not going to be a good morning for that. No time for small talk and politics today. Not when there is a dead body to talk about.*

Deb had just enough time to give Pat a heads-up about Linda's phone call before she spotted Linda pulling up outside in her rusty green Ford pickup. Linda rushed through the doors, looking like a crazy woman. Her normally calm and well-put-together appearance was visibly shaken. Her hair was tousled, she wore no makeup, and her upper lip was taut.

Lord, she looks ten years older, Deb thought. She felt relieved that her wise friend, Pat, was there to help her in this situation. Pat always seemed to know the right thing to say in times of crisis. And today, something was dreadfully wrong in Linda's world.

Deb got up and grabbed a mug from Nathan's waiting hands and threw four bucks on the counter. "I'll need another one today," Deb said, reaching for the second mug. "Keep the change." She turned and called out to Linda, "Have a seat. I'll pour you a cup. What will it be today: dark, light, or decaf?"

"Make it as dark as you can, thanks, and straight up," Linda replied flatly, holding her head in her hands.

Deb rejoined Linda and Pat at the table by the window. Cradling Linda's elbow tenderly, she put the steaming mug down in front of her.

"Thanks, Deb and Pat. I am so glad you're both here," Linda blurted out.

"You sounded really worried. What's going on?" Deb asked.

"It's about Forrest. He was taken into the Sheriff's Department yesterday for questioning about his dad's death. They came to the house and asked him to come in voluntarily, and they took him away in the *squad car*," Linda wailed, breaking down as she said the last word. "Can you believe it?"

"Who came?" Deb asked, trying to understand the facts.

"Stupid Sal and that Detective LeSeur guy," Linda replied.

"Did they arrest him?" Deb asked solicitously.

"No, they let him go. But they kept him there for hours. It took most of the afternoon, and I was beside myself the whole time, trying to think of who I could call—who I could hire to represent him. Even though they did it to me, I still can't believe the police can just take someone away like that, without charging him with a crime. I've learned more about the cops than I ever wanted to know!"

"Well, they can," Deb said matter-of-factly, "if he gave permission. Did he say he wanted to talk to them?"

"Oh, you know Forrest," Linda continued. "He's just so amiable, and he doesn't appreciate the risk. He just said, 'Mom, I have nothing to hide. There is no harm in just talking to them. After all, I know my dad better than almost anyone.' Then he paused and said, 'Knew ... he's dead. Better than anyone but you.' And when Forrest makes up his mind to do something, there's just no stopping him. So he went voluntarily." Linda looked at Deb imploringly.

"But why do you think that Forrest would be of any

serious interest in their investigation?" Pat asked. "You don't possibly think Forrest could have had anything to do with his father's death?"

"Someone must have spilled the beans about Mac and Forrest being at each other," Linda explained.

"What do you mean, 'at each other'?" Deb asked.

"Last September, right after Old Last Night, things came to a head between the two of them. There had been tensions brewing for a while, and then everything sort of just boiled over. They had this huge fight out in the field by the barn. It all happened so fast that it seemed like it came out of nowhere, like a volcano erupting."

"But it's normal for young men to break away from their fathers at Forrest's age. And it's usually not so pretty," Pat stated calmly. "It just doesn't follow that a petty quarrel could lead to such an act of violence. Were you there for this argument? Did Forrest threaten his dad or anything?"

"No, but there was a lot of screaming and yelling. It scared the bejeebers out of me, seeing those two going at it like that. It was just so out of character for both of them."

"What was it about?" Deb asked.

"Oh, Mac was on Forrest's case again about his music. He had invited Forrest a while ago to join the tour and go on the road, but Forrest refused. Said he didn't want to hitch his wagon to Mac's but wanted to make his own way in the world. It was just a lot for Mac to swallow, I guess. I think the guilt just got too much for him. It was probably all those years of being away while Forrest was growing up. It was like all of a sudden those lost years just caught up with him, and he realized that he hadn't had much influence over the kind of man Forrest had become. Trying to turn back the clock, I guess."

Linda held her hands around her cup of coffee, as if to warm them, even on this bright spring day. "The kicker came when Mac made the mistake of dragging me into it; he said that Forrest was still too tied to my apron strings. That was just too much for Forrest. And then Forrest said some mean things, accusing Mac of mistreating me over the years."

"So how did the fight end?" Deb asked. "Did they come to blows?"

"No, just a lot of kicking dust around and strong statements being yelled that neither one of them meant. The last thing I remember is Forrest's yelling at his dad, 'I never want to see you in these parts again!' And then Mac spun his wheels down the road."

"I can see why you're worried, Linda," Pat said consolingly. "But even though it looked and sounded bad, an argument like that still doesn't usually lead to murder. At least, that's how I see it. And I'll bet Sal sees it that way too."

"Did anyone else witness this fight?" Deb asked. She scratched her head.

"Oh, I'm sure there were several people at the Tent site. As I recall, the grounds crew was taking all the equipment out of the backstage area and putting it away for the winter. Phil was there and a few others. They were mostly trying to ignore it all. There were probably three or four others who heard it."

Deb patted Linda's arm reassuringly. "I agree with Pat," she said, hoping to sound convincing. *No way am I going to tell her what I really think. It's such a slippery slope once the police bring you in.* "Let's wait and see if any other information comes out before we panic and assume that Forrest is responsible for Mac's death. Let's just wait and see what the day brings." She patted Linda's arm once more, telling her, "We are glad we could be here for you. I wish we could do more. Call us any time. Anyway, I have a wedding to do today, and you don't," she said to Pat, doing her best to lighten the heavy mood. "I can't believe that I agreed to do weddings for the judge. And Sam is going to be taking the pictures. I just love his work!"

Deb was surprised to see Linda blush at the mention of Sam's name. *I wonder why?* she thought.

"Have fun, Deb, and don't forget—you're meeting me at Carl's house today after your wedding. He wants to talk."

"I'll do my best to be there by three," Deb replied. She gathered up her purse and sweater and prepared to face another Friday by the big lake, leaving Pat and Linda to finish their coffee.

"So," Pat said after Deb's exit, "where do you think Forrest would like to have a little memorial service for his dad? At the church?" She reached over and put her hand on Linda's.

"Well, we talked about it. For me, it's kind of awkward, but some of the people at the Tent really think it would be a good idea. Frankly, I just can't think about it. Life has just gotten so crazy." She sipped from her cup.

"Listen, I know this is a challenge for you. First of all, I want to tell you how much I admire the way you're handling this. Wait a little, if you have to. You can leave most of it in my hands, if you want. I'll talk to the house band. They might be able to play for a service, and I know Carl would read scripture. Trust me. You can call me Monday, and we'll talk about it then. You have enough to handle with Forrest and everything's being up in the air, let alone your own grief."

Linda sniffed. "Thanks for understanding. I don't think anyone realizes that just because we weren't together anymore, that doesn't mean I don't still feel for him, you know?"

"Oh, I do know, and so do all the divorced or separated people in this town. Don't worry. Plenty of people understand and want to help if they can. But for now, let's drink a toast." Pat raised her cup. "To the father of a great son; to

126

a man who could make beautiful music; and to a person we wish to remember with love."

To that, they clinked their cups.

Deb worried as she looked at her watch on the drive to the Marina. *I have to hurry, or I'm going to be late to meet Marc.* The wedding had gone well, after the groom arrived fifteen minutes late. It had been all Deb could do to calm the mother of the bride.

Half an hour later, Deb was struggling to put up the spinnaker pole, fumbling to find the notch for the long metal pipe that Marc had insisted was right in front of her face. Deb shook her hair in the warm breeze.

The wind was 10 to 12 knots, according to Marc; perfect for testing the mettle of the little rocket after a winter of forced rest. Deb never thought in knots; To her it was just a "nice breeze."

"Come on, Deb, you can do it!" urged Marc. "It just snaps on like a cap on a bottle. Then all you have to do is tie a quick bowline knot, and you're all set!"

"A what?" Deb replied anxiously, a look of confusion on her face.

"Oh, Deb, don't tell me you don't remember how. After all those hours we spent practicing with the kids, surely you can remember. They all know how to do it."

"Don't tell me what I should remember!" Deb snapped. "You know how hard all this technical stuff is for my brain. It's just not as easy as it looks." Marc rolled his eyes.

Deb loved being out on the big lake. She loved the light as it sparkled on the waves like miniature diamonds; loved the feel of the breeze caressing her body and the warm sun on her face. She loved the peace and quiet, just the two of them for as far as the eye could see; loved being taken away to a place where they could leave all worries behind.

If only I didn't have to do the grunt work, Deb thought. Despite all their years together and all of Marc's earnest effort, she still had only acquired a rudimentary sense of the art of sailing. *Marc has a PhD in sailing knowledge*, Deb thought, *and I still haven't graduated from kindergarten. And today, it shows.*

Deb closed her eyes, and her mind flashed to the warm blue seas of the tropics ...

She pictured herself on a long sleek houseboat with a crew of three aboard: captain, first mate, and gourmet cook. She was lounging on the deck, smartly dressed in bikini, sunglasses, and sunhat, sipping a margarita. A handsome young chef stepped out of the galley and held out a tray of freshly prepared stuffed shrimp.

Marc sat on the side of the boat, contentedly tending the fishing line he had hanging over the side. Reggae music played softly from the galley.

"Can I do anything for you?" the chef asked solicitously.

Deb sighed and shook her head, feeling the warm sun and breezes on her face. Relaxed ... relaxed ... relaxed.

Suddenly, she felt cold Lake Superior water splashing on her face.

"Just pull on that sheet over there—quick!" Marc said, a note of urgency creeping into his voice.

Sheet? Deb thought frantically. *Is that a sail?* She pulled hard on the edge of the jib, the front sail on the boat, looking back at Marc with a look of triumph on her face.

"No, not that!" Marc said with exasperation. Before he could continue, a head wind came upon them, and the two of them found themselves flying overboard, and *Hot Sauce* turtled upside down in the water.

As Deb hurled backward into the still-chilly waters, she caught a glimpse of Marc being thrown sideways, a look of helpless surprise on his face. Then it was all water.

"Help!" Deb yelled, panic in her voice.

They bobbed like two ducks in water, as they both were wearing their life vests. Marc went immediately into rescue mode. Deb managed to quell her panic, remembering the practice drills Marc had forced her to do so many times with the kids, in order to take away the fear of drowning.

Stay with the boat. Don't let go, she thought, managing to once again swallow a mouthful of water.

Marc was quickly at her side and holding her up. Deb looked at his sopping wet clothes and thought of the absurdity of the two of them floating on top of two hundred feet of water. She burst into laughter.

Marc appeared insulted at first. "So you think this is funny? My boat could be ruined! What about my spinnaker pole?"

"Oh, honey, don't worry. I have so much confidence in you," she cajoled, trying to stop laughing. "Here we are, alive together. At the moment, we own this lake."

A bemused expression crossed Marc's face as he quickly realized that Deb was actually *enjoying* the moment with him; she was enjoying this little sailing disaster, even though her worst fear had been realized. Marc grabbed Deb's hand and pulled her to the turtled boat.

"Come on, mate, let's get this little pot turned over," he said, with a lilt in his voice. He pushed Deb playfully over the top of the boat.

Just as they got *Hot Sauce* righted again, a loud "cigarette"—a sleek racing boat—pulled up next to them. Heinrich Wilson threw them a line.

"Do you need some help?" Heinrich asked. "I saw you go over into the drink."

"No, we'll be fine," Deb assured him. "Marc knows what he's doing. Pretty nice boat you're driving there. Whose boat is that?"

"Mine," Heinrich replied sheepishly, feeling embarrassed about owning such a toy.

"How does a starving artist afford such a monster?" Deb asked, not caring if she seemed nosey. *Did I just say that?* she thought. *Must have been the shock of the cold water.*

"Maybe Monty wasn't the only one with secrets," Heinrich replied mysteriously.

"Thanks for the offer of help," Marc interjected. "We'll be fine. See you on shore!"

Waving good-bye, Heinrich flew off over the waves toward the lighthouse, like an eagle streaking off to a fish.

Chapter Sixteen

While Deb and Marc were drying off, Pat was finishing her visiting for the church. She stopped at home to change into her jeans and T-shirt before heading to Bayfield.

On her phone messages from the night before was yet another frantic call from Carl. He begged her to come over and talk and enticed her with an offer of a great dessert. When she tried to call back, there was no answer and so she left a message for him: "Okay, Carl, I can make it for an hour, but then I have a meeting with a wedding couple at four. See you there. Bye."

And for goodness sake, get a grip! she thought.

Pat arrived at the distinguished white Victorian in Bayfield a little early but didn't see Deb's car there. She debated whether to wait or go on up the steps.

Heck, he can probably see me sitting out here like a fool. Better go in, she thought. She looked in her rearview mirror to quickly check her hair and then got out of her car. The Fifth Symphony was drifting out the window as she climbed the stairs and rang the bell. She waited and then rang again. Still nothing.

Maybe he's got the music so loud that he can't hear the bell. She rang it again. Glancing around, she noticed an elderly man watching her from his window across the street.

I bet nobody gets away with anything on this street, she thought idly. She waved a friendly hand at him, and he dropped the curtain abruptly. *Well, nobody's looking now.*

A brisk breeze off the big lake reminded her it was still spring and that she should have worn her warmer coat.

Br-r-r, let me just ... Turning the handle experimentally, she found it wasn't locked. *Doesn't anyone lock their houses here?* she wondered, shaking her head. *I'll just open it a tiny bit and yell in.* "Hello, Carl? Are you home?"

Except for the music, everything was quiet—until the back door slammed.

Pat stood still. She knew the layout of this particular house. If she was right, the door to the kitchen was close off to the right. *Someone must be there—or has just left. Where is Deb? Should I just walk in?*

"Friend of mine, are you holding that door open so the flies can get in or what?"

Heart pounding, Pat turned to see Deb right behind her. "Gosh, you scared me," she panted, catching her breath.

"Sorry. But why don't you go in? Where's Carl?"

"I don't know," Pat whispered. "But I heard a door in the back slam. I think someone was in there, and I scared them off."

"Stop it. This is Bayfield, for goodness sake. Not the big

132

city. Carl probably just didn't hear you come in. Let's go see."

Pat put out her hand to stop Deb. "I don't know. I have a bad feeling."

Deb pushed past her and walked briskly across the floor to the kitchen calling out, "Carl, we're here!" She called to Pat from the kitchen entry. "No one in here, Miss Heebie-Jeebie."

Pat waited for her heart to stop beating like an Irish drum as she looked around in awe. Every single spot was filled with vases, Victorian furniture, and knick-knacks.

What would my mother, the antique dealer, say if she saw this? Pat thought. She walked into the hall and then the kitchen, where she saw that the coffee was on. The table was set. *With those cute little matching luncheon plates*, Pat noted. But no Carl.

"He probably just stepped out to get something. Don't worry about it," Deb stage-whispered.

"Or I scared someone away when I came in," Pat insisted, also in a whisper. "And if you're not worried, why are you whispering? Don't you wish now you had bought an extra mace when you got one for Julia at college?"

Making a face at Pat, Deb was saved from replying as a voice called to them from upstairs.

"Oh, hello, girls. I didn't hear you ring." A smiling Carl came down the ornately carved staircase. "I've got a great dessert from Racheli's. Let's eat and talk."

Pat pulled out a chair and settled in for a good gossip, but she couldn't stop wondering, *Who went out the door?* She turned to Carl and said admiringly, "Carl, you know I've never been inside your lovely house before, but wow, you are really a collector!"

"Sorry about not having you over sooner," he apologized. "I don't entertain here much. But actually, I'm not much of a collector," he said as he watched Pat look around the kitchen.

Pat noticed an early pie cabinet, and inside the screen doors was a collection of Majolica dishes and serving plates to die for. She pushed back from the table and went over to the beautiful dry sink. "This is original, isn't it?" she said appreciatively. She ran her hand along it and noticed a collection of hog-scraper candlesticks inside it, along with some pewter measurers that she was sure were Early American. "Don't try to kid the daughter of an antique dealer. This collection is wonderful."

"Collection?" Carl looked puzzled and then smiled. "No, this isn't my collection. It's actually my mom's. She was the one who got all this. Over the years she became the favorite of the local dealers. The money she would spend! That pie safe took me on quite an adventure when I was a teen. The two of us picked it up in North Dakota. With the cost of gas and truck rental, it cost a small fortune. But once she wanted something, she just had to have it. To me it just looks like home."

"So, do you collect something else?" Pat asked. "Let me guess. Stamps? You're a philatelist!"

"Nope," Carl answered.

"Come on. Children of collectors never fall far from the tree. Let's see … could it be books? I love them myself," she persisted.

Carl just looked at her.

"Paintings? Great art? Do you have a stunning collection hidden away in a temperature-controlled room?"

"No, really, I don't collect. Look around you. There isn't room for my own stuff."

"Maybe it's upstairs," Pat suggested, taking a step toward the stairs. "'Fess up. I'm an antique dealer's daughter so I know it runs in the blood." She was clearly teasing him, but one look at Carl's stony face made her stop in her tracks. *What in the world?*

Carl cleared his throat. "No, really, the Tent is my personal life. I have collected a few pieces over the years—gifts, you understand. But that's about it. Come on. Coffee is ready."

Pat looked around the small pink-and-green kitchen that had been so popular in the fifties. The room contained evidence of the best of that era. There were four-inch tiles on the counters and backsplash, black-and-white twelve-inch tiles on the floor, and even a pink stove. The deep soapstone sink fit right in. Above the kitchen table and chairs on the wall was an early autographed poster of Willie Nelson, looking out of place in the grand old kitchen. "I knew you collected!" she crowed, sitting down at the walnut drop-leaf table.

"Yes," he said proudly, "a few of the artists have given me small gifts. And you are right. I do have a collection, of sorts. If you're interested some time, I'll share a few with you."

"That would be great," Deb said. *Come on guys, I've got places to go, things to do,* she thought impatiently. "So Carl, what do you make of all this?" Deb asked, trying to bring them back to the subject at hand. "Do you have any ideas of who would have killed Monty?"

"Should I play Mother?" Pat asked, settling in at the table. She poured out the coffee, and Carl absentmindedly put two sugar cubes in his cup.

"I just don't know," he said, "I've stayed up practically all night, trying to figure it out. It just can't be Linda or Forrest. I just know it in my soul." He dramatically touched his heart. Leaning forward to take the cream Pat handed him, he continued. "There has been some talk about drugs. Could it have been that?"

Shades of a small town, Pat thought. *How did he hear that already?*

"Maybe," Deb said tentatively. "But why would Mac be killed because of it? If he was bringing in drugs, it seems that it would be a reason to keep him alive—so that he could bring in more when he traveled this year."

"Oh, I don't know. Maybe someone didn't get his cut. Maybe Mac tried to keep someone's money and that person got mad. It could have happened," Carl said. "Not that I have any proof or anything," he added, noticing their skeptical faces. "Still, it would be nice if it was someone we didn't know, wouldn't it? But if money is the motive, then how about the band members? I heard Heinrich, his drummer, complaining about being cheated. How about him?"

"If we're talking money, could it be Linda? I'll bet he never paid child support," Pat suggested as she took a cookie from the tray.

Carl stopped pouring himself a second cup. "No, not Linda!" he said, spilling the coffee into his saucer. "I just know she wouldn't do it."

"Someone said she has a temper," Pat said, playing devil's advocate. "More than one person has felt her wrath. I'm just saying, money is a motive. And the other motive for murder applies to her, too." She took a big bite of the cucumber sandwiches Carl had put out. *These are wonderful*, she thought. *Whoever takes the time to cut off crusts and make these little cute sandwiches anymore?* She savored it, knowing she wouldn't allow herself to take another. "A minute on the lips, a month on the hips" was her mantra these days.

"What other motive?" he asked.

"Well ... love ... sex," Deb replied. "And she might have that motive. We really can't rule her out," she added apologetically, patting his hand. "We can't just leave people out because we like them."

"Maybe not, but then you'd have to add a dozen young beauties from the bay area."

"What do you mean?" Deb asked. "Do you have some names?"

"I might be able to give you some. He was quite a womanizer, you know."

"I've heard that, but strangely, the women I've talked to liked him anyway. The guy really had that Scottish charm," Deb said. "The only one who was really mad was the one he stood up on Old Last Night."

"It really was his 'old last night,' wasn't it?" Carl laughed nervously. "Sorry," he added hastily. "I don't know what has gotten into me. Frankly, I hated him!"

Pat carefully put her cup down on its saucer. She wiped her lips with the vintage linen hardanger napkin. "That's a pretty strong feeling, Carl. Is there something you want to tell us?"

As if regretting his outburst, Carl chewed on his lip and then said, "No, I mean I hate what he's done to my Big Top, that's all."

I'm sure that's true, Pat thought, giving Deb a knowing look. *But for sure that's not all of the truth.*

Carl looked pointedly at his watch. "Oh, my gosh, where has the time gone?" he asked. "Sorry, but I really have to get to a board meeting. We're discussing what all this will do to the finances. Just keep me informed, will you? And thanks again for coming over."

Well, that's a brush off if I ever heard one, Deb thought, picking up her purse.

As they stepped out onto the porch, she turned to Pat. "Got a client. Got to run. Remember, it's Ballyhoo night, and we are serving beer."

"And I've got a visit with a dear old man here in Bay-field," Pat said. "See you later."

As she got in her car, Pat looked back across the street and saw the man in the window, watching the neighborhood once again.

On the drive home from her visit in Bayfield, Pat suddenly decided that she should get a look at the barn in the daylight. *Maybe it'll give me some ideas.*

There was no sign of the green pickup as she passed Linda's house, and for that, she was glad. *I don't want to explain what I'm doing here, especially since I don't know myself.* She drove up to the outbuilding and parked on the dirt road, then sat for a minute, enjoying the quiet.

It wasn't hard for her to miss the yellow crime-scene tape on the doors and the surrounding area. "You dummy, Pat," she said aloud, banging her hand on the steering wheel. "You should have known you couldn't go in."

Maybe I can just walk around the outside. I need to stretch my legs anyway. She got out of the car and walked around the wooded side of the barn, softly humming to herself. She forgot for a moment where she was—or the reason she was here—as she enjoyed the budding trees and smell of spring.

This is silly, she admonished herself as she rounded the building. *If anyone catches me out here, what will I say? "I'm looking for the killer to come back to the scene of the crime, just like in an old Sherlock Holmes novel"?*

Just then a loud banging from the other side of the building stopped her cold. *What the heck? Maybe the killer does come back to the scene.* Before she could plan her next move, Heinrich walked around the corner of the building.

"What are you doing here?" he demanded.

"*Me?*" she said, more bravely than she felt. "I could ask you the same thing. You didn't go inside, did you? It's still a crime scene, you know." *That's just great, Pat*, she thought. *Make the stranger in the woods angry.*

"Hell, no." He took a step toward her, then stopped and smiled sheepishly. "No, I didn't, but I thought about it.

No, I'm just trying to get some closure is all. Still can't believe Mac's been dead all this time and I didn't even know." He rubbed his chin. "How about you?"

"About the same," Pat admitted. "Just trying to get a better handle on what happened, I guess."

"Well, I'd better get going. That wet-behind-the-ears detective asked me to drop by for an interview. Imagine a police detective in a big city ever asking you politely to drop by," he said, shaking his head. Without another word, he walked away.

Looking for closure, or was it something else he was looking for? Maybe a left-behind murder weapon? I wonder if a drumstick could crush in a nose, Pat wondered as she watched him leave. Shuddering at the thought, she quickly walked back to her car. After starting the engine, she locked the doors. *Just in case.*

Later that night, with Deb at the wheel of her white Prius, Pat scanned the gravel parking lot in front of the big blue tent. "Wow, there are already a lot of cars here. Are we late?" she asked.

Deb pulled neatly into her parking spot between two SUVs. "Please turn left at the next corner," said a disembodied voice. "That darn GPS," Deb griped. "I must have knocked the 'on' button."

Pat giggled, and the men in the backseat laughed out loud.

Marc had given her the navigating system last Christmas, because the two women were notorious for getting lost. Somehow it hadn't helped. Pat kept imagining a little person pulling out her hair, as time after time the friends didn't listen to its advice. She giggled again.

"Anyway, no. We're actually early for a change," Deb said. "But I guess people are turning out for Ballyhoo night to show support in trying times."

"Or else," Marc said in his best Dracula voice, "it's in order to get the latest scoop on the murder."

Deb rolled her eyes and released her seatbelt. She stuck her keys carefully in her coat pocket. Lately, it had been as if keys and other small items were walking away on their own. Marc said it was menopausal. *What does he know, anyway? He's only a doctor.*

"Whatever reason, we had better get to the beer truck. You know how the beermeister loves to train us beer maids."

The two men got out of the backseat, laughing between themselves.

"See you later," they said, waving as they went off to grill brats for the huge crowd.

"Ballyhoo!" the two women shouted after them.

As they walked to the beer wagon, Mary Jo from the Ashland Chamber of Commerce greeted them with a smile. "Got any beer yet? I'm ready!" she said enthusiastically. Mary Jo was one of the faithful regulars on Ballyhoo night.

"How did this night get started anyway, Deb?" Pat asked, following Deb and Mary Jo to the beer wagon.

"Oh, as Mary Jo here knows well by now," Deb replied patiently, "it's a chance for Big Top to seduce Chamber types with free food and beer so that they can keep feeding those patrons into the ticket office all summer long. Besides, who can resist the allure of beer-soaked brats, all the beer and root beer floats you can drink, and fabulous entertainment under balmy skies in a setting like this?" Deb waved her arms around. "And topped off by a free show by the Blue Canvas Orchestra, the house band."

"What's the show tonight?" Mary Jo asked.

"Why, it's Best of the Big Top, of course," Deb replied with a smile. She picked up a blue apron from the table and put it on.

Mary Jo handed Deb some official-looking papers. "These are for you. Carolyn asked me to drop them off." With a wave, she was off to the grills, where the men had already started the brats. "Are you ready for the crowds?" she yelled ahead of her.

Pat moved the papers to a serving table so there would be room for all the free glasses of beer they were going to fill.

Carolyn walked up and handed Pat some pens. "Hey, Pat, please leave those papers out here. Those are surveys so people can give their opinion."

"Opinions on what?" Deb asked, as she continued to pour glasses of Leinie's beer.

"Oh, you remember the bronze statue idea? Well, we're trying to decide who should be a part of the sculpture, and so we're asking patrons. The beer tables seemed the logical place."

"Good idea, right?" Pat looked everywhere but at Deb, because she knew if she did, she would start laughing. "Okay, Carolyn," Pat agreed, "we'll put them right here in front, so everyone can see them."

Carolyn nodded and then walked briskly away, moving on to her next task.

"Don't blame me if they're covered with beer at the end of the night or if the names become funnier as they drink more," Pat muttered to Deb. Luckily, Carolyn didn't hear Pat's whisper or at least chose not to.

"Give away enough free beers, and they'll be writing our names down!" Deb giggled. "Would I look thinner in bronze?" she asked, striking a pose.

Pat just laughed and filled another glass from the tap.

"Whew! How do you think a hot flash would show up in bronze?" Deb asked, fanning her face.

Pat laughed again, not bothering to answer. They were startled by a booming voice behind them.

"And remember to tip the glass slightly as you pull the tap," the jovial beermeister said as he poured each of them a tall glass of the new spring special brew. "This year, we named it Big Top Ballyhoo."

"Ballyhoo!" they shouted together and each took a sip.

"So," the beermeister said after they had savored the new brew for a moment. "What have you found out about the murder? Were you really there, and did you find the body?"

"Let's see," Deb said, still savoring her beer. "I really don't know if we should talk about it."

Pat gave her a nudge. *After all, he might have information of his own to share.*

"I really liked Mac," he went on, taking another sip. "He always came to Ballyhoo, walking through the crowds, signing autographs. One time, a few years back, I remember him even helping out at this very table, pouring free beers. Of course, his lines filled up with all the pretty girls." His eye twinkled as he remembered. "That man sure had an eye for the ladies. I would say his murderer was a jealous husband, but he was pretty honorable, in his way. No, seems to me he had his pick of the young eligibles. No need to steal from another man's stable. I don't get it," he said, shaking his head. "You know everyone liked the guy. What do you think?"

"I think the crowds are getting restless," Deb answered. "What say we open up and give away some beer?"

"Right on," Pat agreed.

As they started pouring, the noise from the happy

crowd could be heard all the way up to the top of the ski hill.

"Oh, look, it's the raffle-ticket ladies!" a young woman said as she approached the table. "Two bucks, two bucks, two bucks!" she sang out, imitating their well-known technique.

"Ballyhoo," Deb and Pat said in chorus.

The Tent season was definitely rolling, even though curiosity about Mac's death was running like a wild moose through the crowd.

It's a comfort to know, thought Deb, *that the show will indeed go on.*

Chapter Seventeen

The Tent was unusually packed that night, and the music was lively and energizing.

At the end of the show, as the stage lights dimmed and the last strains drifted into the air like wisps of sweet perfume, the crowd erupted into enthusiastic applause. Waiting for the traditional, obligatory encore, the well-trained crowd settled back into their church-pew seats.

But instead of the typical quiet song, Deb and Pat were surprised when Ed strolled onto the stage and took the mike, saying, "We have a special encore tonight in tribute to the late Monty McIntyre, and in honor of the circle of people coming to the Tent. There will never be an unbroken circle at the Big Top." Raising his arms like a band director and urging the crowd to join in, Ed led the house band in a rousing chorus of "Will the Circle Be Unbroken?"

Will the circle be unbroken?
By and by Lord, by and by?
There's a better life awaiting,
In the sky, Lord, in the sky.

"Come on up on stage! Make a circle with us! Anyone who wants, come join us!" Ed's sweet voice implored.

"Come on, Pat. Now's our chance to be on stage!" Deb gestured excitedly, pointing to the growing numbers of happy audience members who were dancing up to the front to the beat of the music.

"Not me. I'm not making a fool of myself," Pat replied.

"Since when did that ever stop you?" Deb retorted. "This is nothing like the time we did the hula on the stage in Maui, for heaven's sake!"

Pat sighed resignedly and followed Deb up to the stage, amid the growing frenzy and insistent rhythm of the melody. The circle of community began growing exponentially, filling in with local friends and neighbors. Pat looked around the circle as she reached her hand out to a gray-haired gentleman who skipped his way to join them, a look of childlike wonder on his face.

Pat recognized so many faces in the crowd. There was Linda, and there was Forrest, trying hard to avoid looking toward his mother. There was Phil, the operations manager, looking happier and more relaxed than before Mac's body had been found. There was Carl, looking a bit awkward, trying to keep the beat with his foot but falling a step or two behind. And of course, there was Ed and Cheryl, the two Bruces, Tom, Jack, Cal, and Andy, all letting themselves go and giving into the Tent magic. The energy was almost enough to lift Pat off her feet.

Smiling, Deb's heart skipped a beat as she noticed Marc and Mitch also coming on stage. Pat saw Sam in the crowd. The classy photographer was positively beaming, caught up in the excitement of the moment and enjoying the close-knit camaraderie that had been conjured. Pat looked closer and noticed that tears were trickling down Sam's face.

Pat nudged Deb and nodded in Sam's direction. Deb gave Pat a quizzical look in return.

It's nights like this—unbelievable nights of community and musical unity and magic—that must keep the band going year after year, Deb thought. She sighed, losing herself in the music and looked again at the faces in the circle, as she silently thanked her lucky stars for the gift of that moment.

Picking up the phone by the third ring was second-nature to Pat. A pastor of twenty-some years, she had acquired the same skill that she imagined doctors must have—to awaken instantly for calls in the middle of the night. So when the phone rang late that night, Pat instinctively reached for it, causing the book she'd fallen asleep reading to hit the floor with a thump. Looking at the clock, she saw that it was 12:30 a.m. She cleared her throat and said into the receiver, "Hello, this is Pastor Pat."

"Wha-at? I'm ... I'm sure sorry. I guess I've got the wrong number."

"Who are you calling?" Pat asked politely. She could tell only that the person on the other end was young and male.

"Is ... is this the Pat that volunteers at the tent?"

"Yes, it is," Pat answered, sitting up straighter in bed against her propped pillows. "Who is this, please?"

"Darn, it's later than I thought," the voice mumbled.

He sounded even sorrier now, as if it had been a mistake to call. "Sorry. Maybe I should call back another time."

"Wait," Pat said quickly as she tried to identify the familiar-sounding voice. "It's not that late. I was just reading." *Yeah, reading while I snored*, she thought. "Is this ... Forrest?" she asked.

"It's me, Forrest," said the voice on the phone.

Reassuringly, Pat added, "Don't worry about the time or the pastor thing. Can I help you with anything? Is your mom all right?"

There was a pause and Pat could almost hear him thinking it had been a mistake to call. But she knew that he had to decide for himself to continue, so she waited.

"Yeah," Forrest sighed. "It's me, and yes, Mom is okay—for now, I guess. Gosh, I forgot you were a preacher, but it makes sense." A little of his natural good humor showed through. "You really are good at talking people into stuff."

Pat laughed with him and settled back, knowing he had decided to talk. "This has been a hard time for you, hasn't it, Forrest?"

"Man, you can't believe how hard," he agreed. "He wasn't always around ... he traveled a lot you know. My dad, I mean. We didn't always get along, not even about music. But, he was my dad, you know ..." His voice trailed off. "And now we'll never have time. I just keep thinking if I had only told him how great I really thought he was ..."

"Your dad did love you, Forrest. Anyone who saw the two of you together saw that." Pat waited, letting the silence fill the space between them.

"Anyway," he said, clearing his throat. "That's why I called. Sort of. I need some advice. Hey, if you're a pastor, does that mean this is confidential, like with priests?"

"It is, but formal confession is the only place I can't ever tell what you say. Is that what this is, Forrest? A confession?" Her heart skipped a beat, hoping that it wasn't. She liked this young musician.

"*What?* Heck, no! I mean, I didn't kill him. Is that what you think? No, I'm calling about my mom. You seem to get along with her, what with you both being quilters and all. And I wondered … could you maybe talk to her? I just don't want you to tell her I called."

She breathed a sigh of relief. "Sure, if you want. Anything specific you have in mind?" Pat asked, remembering the conversation with Linda just twelve hours before. "Actually, I have talked to her. Deb and I met her for coffee this morning." *It seems like such a long time ago*, she thought.

"Oh, so that's where she went." He seemed relieved. "Truth is, I'm scared half out of my mind. She had fights with him, you know. His wandering … never being able to settle down. He just wasn't the kind, I guess." There was a pause. "It was one of the reasons they never married. And sometimes, she would get so hurt and angry."

"Young man, are you worried about whether she …" Pat stopped, grasping for just the right word. "That she got so angry, she might have done something?"

"No, of course not," Forrest answered almost too quickly. "She's just… you know … so easy to pin it on, being the one closest to him and all. Everyone at the Tent knows how mad she can get, but she wouldn't have, see, because in her way, she loved him still."

A great motive for a crime of passion, Pat thought. "So why call me? You sound worried. And you know what? She sounded worried this morning, too—about you."

"She was? About me?" he answered in wonder. "Just be her friend, is all. Don't let her do or say anything stupid she'll regret."

The age-old question, Pat thought. *Am I my brother's—or in this case, my sister's—keeper?*

"Forrest," she said, gently but firmly, "your mom is a great woman. Tell her you're worried and scared. My advice? Talk to her, not me. I actually gave her the same advice. But don't call her tonight. You know she is in bed as soon as the sun goes down. And try not to worry."

"I know, I know," he moaned. "But how does a guy tell his mom when he's worried she killed his dad?"

For that, Pat didn't have an answer.

Chapter Eighteen

"It's going to be okay; it's going to be ..."

Rocking the old white chair back and forth on it back legs, his mantra went on.

Funny ... I thought once they found it, I would be free of it, but time after time, I find myself in this place, in this chair, waiting.

Waiting for? Forgiveness? Or to just be found out at last? The killer always returns. I never understood that, but now I do. I return, hoping against all hope that it was all a bad dream, and it didn't happen at all.

It's going to be ... Angrily, he stood up, picked up the old chair, and smashed it to bits. *It's never going to be okay again!*

Chapter Nineteen

Getting up for church the next day was a little harder for Pat than usual. *Give me strength to do the best I can, Lord. I may be tired, but there might be someone who needs to hear a good word.* Pat's prayer was not unusual as she drove over to the church for the eight-thirty morning service. She and God had a deal: she didn't try to get flowery when asking for help, and God … well, God always took her as she was.

Esther pulled up right beside her as Pat got out of her car. *Good and faithful Esther would understand.* "Hey, kiddo, good morning. Say, could you take the announcements today? Frankly, if I were a snowmobile, I would be running on fumes."

Esther nodded sympathetically. "Hard night?"

"Late calls. Oh, and would you say something in the prayers for Linda and Forrest and Mac?"

"No problem," Esther said as they walked together toward the door.

This must be why Jesus sent people out two by two, Pat thought gratefully. *Thanks, God.*

Esther walked up to the lectern and smiled. "Welcome, everyone! It's so nice to see guests in our midst." She peered out over the large podium as if she was greeting everyone individually. Her long dark braid hung down her back and swayed slightly as she leaned forward. "And of course, you are all welcome to coffee time after worship. No Lutheran's Sunday would feel complete without it." There were polite snickers from the pews.

"On a sadder note, you will notice in the prayers today we will lift up the friends and family of Monty McIntyre. There will be a small memorial service next week. I'm sure everyone will contribute cookies and cakes for a coffee time afterward." She raised her voice above the murmurs. "I know many of us have loved his music at the Tent over the years. Keep them in your daily prayers, please." She looked down at her notes and then continued, "Oh, and don't forget your recipes for the church cookbook. We can't make it without you, and all the proceeds will go to our Circle of Grace Program," she gently encouraged them. "And now, let's do what we've come here for—worship." She stepped back, nodding at Pat to begin.

The service went pretty well, Pat thought as she greeted worshippers in the back of the sanctuary an hour later. The time after the service was always a favorite of hers. There was the baby boy that she had baptized two years ago, coming with Grandma. *Boy, can he run now!* And the widower who had been married for seventy-two years before losing his wife. *Imagine that!*, Pat thought as they exchanged hugs. Person after person—she had grown to love each of them and knew they cared about her, too.

Next came Forrest. He looked so young and vulnerable.

"Thanks, Pat, and you, too, Esther, for mentioning my dad and the prayers." He looked uncomfortable, like he didn't know what to do next. His mother came up behind him and put her hand on his shoulder.

"I'll call you tomorrow, if it's okay," Linda said quietly. "Mac had no family except this great kid here. His parents are gone. I guess they're with him now, right?" She wiped her eyes, as if to clear them of sadness. "Anyway, thanks for ... well, for everything."

Following her lanky son, she walked out the door. And since church people are still people after all, the crowd around the coffee all watched them go.

Chapter Twenty

The next morning, Deb glanced across the mahogany table in her conference room at the cute blonde sprite with pigtails and a missing front tooth. Amanda Thompson was the picture of childhood innocence.

"Well, honey, how has it been going, now that your parents are divorced?" Deb asked. She pushed a plate of cookies toward her.

"They're behaving really good," Amanda replied, "especially now that they got called into the principal's office and the judge told them to behave!" She carefully looked at the cookies and then chose one, popping the whole thing in her mouth.

Deb smiled at the innocent charm of her words. *Out of the mouths of babes,* she mused.

"Deb, are my parents going to get a detention if they don't behave?" Amanda asked plaintively.

Oh, were it so! "Sorry, Amanda, but I'll tell you what:

if they don't behave maybe we'll have to give them some extra homework."

Amanda smiled gratefully, and Deb couldn't keep herself from gently wiping the chocolate off the little girl's face. Reaching in the folder on the table, she offered Amanda her business card. "This is just for you. It's my phone number, here and at home. If you need to talk to someone, call any time."

If only all my clients were so easy to handle, Deb thought.

A day off! Pat put her feet up and opened up the mystery book she had stashed in the seat cushion of her favorite chair. *Now if the phone just doesn't—*

No sooner had the thought popped into her head than her cell rang. *This better be important*, she thought less than charitably, as she marked her place.

"Hello, this is Pastor Pat."

"Hi, Pat. This is Linda. Remember I said I would call today about the memorial service?"

"Of course. I thought I might hear from you today," she replied, feeling guilty for her mean-spirited private thoughts. "Do you want to meet me at the church or just talk on the phone?"

"Oh, no, not at the church. I know it's your day off. I just wanted to touch base with you. Can you plan something for this next week? The coroner has released the body. The house band said they'd play, and Forrest just can't seem to deal with this part at all. He really is just a kid yet."

"Let's plan it for Thursday afternoon, then. That will probably be easier for everyone. How about one o'clock?

"Sounds good. Do you think the ladies will be able to make a lunch?"

"Probably not a lunch." *Like that would happen.* "But I'm sure they'd be more than happy to serve coffee and cake. Does that sound all right?"

"Okay by me. Should I call Esther Marie?"

"Don't bother. You have enough on your plate. I'll take care of that, and Wendy will make sure it gets in the paper. Do you want me to run the service by you before I print it?"

"No, please just do it. And if you could make it a kind of celebration of his life, that would seem more meaningful for us."

"You bet. And Linda, if there's anything else …"

"Thanks, Pat. I know you mean it. Just try to solve this thing will you? Before we all go crazy."

I guess this mystery will just have to wait, Pat thought, putting her book aside. *At least the fictional one.*

That night, the best friends pulled into the Tent parking lot with Deb's boys.

"Thanks, boys, for coming with us again," Pat called into the backseat. "It is a real treat to see the legend Willie Nelson."

"You buy the food, I come," Eric replied.

The food-service people were busy serving the early patrons. One of the pleasures of the Tent was to come early for shows, just to sit leisurely in the nice weather at the picnic tables and have a sandwich and a beer or two. Pat looked over at the table reserved for volunteers—it was already filling up with ticket sellers, car-lot organizers, and ushers who were getting a quick bite before beginning their chores. Music was playing over the PA system. Pat recognized Willie Nelson's famous Stardust bus as she, Deb, Eric, and Bruno wound their way up to the food counter.

"What'll it be?" the smiling woman asked Eric and Bruno. "Eating fish boil tonight?"

The two teens didn't hear because they were arguing about cars.

"Two grilled chicken salads," Deb said. "And two beers," Deb and Pat said at once. "Jinx!" they both added, turning to each other with a smile. Deb turned back to the boys. "Stop the car talk and answer the nice woman."

"Oh, sorry, Mom. Burger basket for me and my friend here." Eric smiled at the server. He turned back to Bruno. "Say whatever you want. You'll never convince me the Beemer isn't the greatest car."

"Boys!" said the server, shaking her head as she watched them walk away. "Boys and cars. What a love affair. Do you know what they want to drink?"

"Make it two Cokes," Deb answered. "Sorry about that."

"Hey, I've got boys of my own. Say! Carl was looking for you two a minute ago. Said to meet him in the star RV. You must really rate," she said a little enviously.

Pat and Deb looked at each other. "Boys, we're taking our food to meet Carl," Deb called out. "Be good."

The boys, busy talking about driver's license requirements in different countries while scoping the crowd for girls, didn't bother to answer.

"I've always wondered what the RV looks like inside," Pat admitted, juggling her food and drink as she walked. "Is it a palace on wheels?"

"Maybe," Deb replied. "Whatever it is, we'll soon find out. It's a good thing that it's only good old Carl we're meeting, because in one of those old mysteries you love to read, this is where the killer would get us."

"Nah, he would have gotten us already, in his kitchen with the carving knife!" Pat joked.

They laughed companionably as they walked out to the field where the trailer was parked.

Pat sobered and looked at Deb. "Except I don't think the killer is ever a portly older Swede, like Carl. What's he going to do? Tie us both up?"

The motorhome door was open, even though it was a cool night, as if he had been watching for them. "Good of you to come," he said jovially. "I see you brought your dinner. Me, too. Here, come on in and sit at the table, where famous people have eaten their favorite foods—everything from oysters to peanut butter and jelly sandwiches. We really do try to give them what they want before a performance." He held the screen door open for them.

"Are you sure we can come in?" Pat asked as she hesitated on the step. "Won't Willie mind?"

"Willie? Why would—oh, I see. Willie doesn't use this one. He brings his own. But don't be too disappointed," he said, seeing their faces fall. "Plenty of other stars have used it. Here, pull up a chair. Need a fork or anything?"

"No, we've got the good old plastic stuff with us," Deb said, waggling her plastic fork in the air. Her eyes drank in all the treasures in the trailer. "Wow! Are these real signatures of people who have stayed here?" She moved over to a board on a wall. "Garrison Keillor, B.B. King, Joan Baez … look, Pat, here's Waylon Jennings. And who's this? I can't make it out."

"Where?" asked Carl, coming over to stand behind her. "Oh, that's the Chinese acrobats. They didn't all actually stay in here overnight, of course. Come on; you can look later. Let's sit and eat, and you can fill me in."

"Oh, darn, I forgot napkins," Pat said as she sat down.

"Can I move this roll of tape?" She picked up a large roll of duct tape that was on the table.

"Now what in the world is that doing here?" Carl asked. "I'm going to have to talk to the crew about using this place, I can see. Sure, let me put it on the counter. And here are some napkins, compliments of the house." With a flourish he took them out of a drawer.

"You really know your way around this bus. How come?" Deb asked.

"Actually, I helped pick this baby out." He patted the wall fondly, as if it were a pet, and then joined them at the table. "Yes, sir, even put some of my own money into her." He leaned forward on his elbows, forgetting about his food. "Nothing's too good for the Tent. I've been with it from the beginning, you know. It's been my constant through several jobs and several wives." He smiled, and sat up once more, picking up his fork.

"This is an important part of Americana, a piece of living history. Nobody should be able to hurt it. That's why this … this disturbance is so irritating." His face flushed and he grew visibly agitated. "Nobody!" He banged his hand on the table while still holding the fork, and food flew toward Pat.

Wow, what's gotten into him? Pat thought. She was taken aback by his outburst but didn't react to it. Instead, she wiped mayonnaise off the table in front of her and asked quietly, "Is that why you asked us here, Carl? Because this death might threaten your place at the Tent? Don't you want to know who killed Mac? To see justice done?"

"Huh?" Carl looked at her, startled by his own reaction. He seemed a million miles away, as if he had forgotten they were there. "Oh, right. Forgive my soapbox. I just love this place." He picked up his sandwich and took a bite. "So what have you learned?" he asked with his mouth full. "Any ideas on who did in the victim?"

"Mac," Pat corrected. "Mac was his name. You knew him well, didn't you?"

"Of course ... I just meant ... it's hard to think of it as someone I knew."

"I heard you had been friends at the beginning—you, Linda, and Mac. But you had a falling out; is that right?"

"No, well, yes, sort of. The Fiddlers were one of the first big acts we had booked at the Tent. And I got to know them. But Mac started running around on Linda right away. I hated that. You can understand—a man with a woman pregnant. And Linda is a wonderful girl—woman, I mean. Everyone liked Linda. Half the guys were in love with her."

"Were you?" Deb asked quietly.

"Was I? What?" He looked google-eyed at Deb. "In love with Linda?" His face flushed again, and the women imagined his blood pressure was rising.

Looks like he's gonna blow, Pat thought. But outwardly, she appeared mild as she looked him straight in the eyes. "Well?"

There was silence in the bus, and then Carl sat back in his chair as he tried to smile and only half succeeded. "Of course. You're investigating. Natural to ask questions, even of me. Otherwise, it wouldn't be thorough, now, would it? Let me see ... it was so long ago." He paused as if trying to remember, but the friends weren't buying whatever he was selling. Deb kicked Pat under the table.

He remembers, all right, Deb thought, *or he wouldn't have gotten so upset.*

"Sure, I guess I was half in love with her then, like most of the boys. We were young hot-bloods. But to answer your question properly, I felt protective of her."

Once again it grew quiet, but Pat kept probing.

She's like someone with a sore tooth, Deb thought, *who can't keep her tongue from touching the aching spot.*

163

"But you didn't like him much, did you?" Pat asked. "All these years, and you've tried to fill in for him with Forrest. You know, anger can be a great motivator; it can cause us problems sometimes, if we keep it all in. So, Carl, what was it like to play second fiddle in a woman's affections, huh? And what's it like to always be taken for granted?"

Deb looked at Pat like she had lost her marbles. Here was the guy who had asked them to look into the murder, and she was ... *What is it that she's doing*?

"What is this?" he demanded. "I've come to help, to cooperate, to save the Tent from disgrace. And you ... are you using some kind of pop psychology on me? Accusing me? Me, who loves this place?" He turned to Deb, looking for rescue. "Deb, you know me. You were board president before me. You tell her."

But Deb was speechless. *I don't know where she's going with this,* she thought, *but I think our guest passes to this bus are gone from now on.*

He rose abruptly from the table, almost knocking over his chair. "Well, just never mind. It was stupid of me to trust two crazy meddling women with something so important. I thought we were friends, Deb. Good day, ladies—and I use the term loosely. Close the door when you're done. And I needn't remind you," he said over his shoulder, "that some of these things in here are priceless ... *and* they're accounted for!" Sticking his cap firmly on his mop of gray hair, he stomped out of the door, slamming it so hard it was heard all the way to the food tent.

The two women stared silently at each other, and then Pat picked up her fork and speared a piece of chicken.

"Well, that was interesting," Pat said.

"Better look at everything in here, because my bet is we'll never see the inside of this baby again," Deb grumbled. Taking a bite of her salad, she looked at her friend and smiled. "Accounted for? Do we look like thieves?" A thoughtful expression came over her face as she looked around the room. "You know, I just thought of something. Some of this stuff is worth some dough. What do you think?"

Pat stopped eating and looked around appraisingly. "Depends. Actually, we never thought of it from that angle. Now that you mention it, there are lots of items that really might be collectors' items."

A sudden bang on the door startled her so much, she spilled her coffee.

"Hallo! Anyone in?"

"Come on in," Deb called out, recognizing the voice. "But if you're looking for Willie, he is in his own trailer."

The door opened, letting in a cool breeze and a hairy bear of a man. "Good. Someone said I'd find you two here," Jack said, smiling behind his bushy beard. "Say, could you help me out? At the pre-show I'm doing some joke magic tricks, and Phil said you two were good sports."

"What do you need?" Pat asked, putting down her cup.

"Well, it's a little silly, but I sort of use these handcuffs to lock you to your chairs." He showed them two sets of handcuffs. "And the house band does some jokes about you two ..." He saw the look of concern on their faces and hastily added, "It's all in good fun. Then, after the laughs, I pretend the trick doesn't work. I can't get you out, and I shrug and walk off stage. Laugh, laugh, and laugh. Pat, you struggle, but Deb, you just yawn and calmly reach over and touch the cuff here." He pointed to a spot. "And presto, they fall off. You take the tape off your mouth, leaving Pat's on. Oh, did I forget to mention the tape? And bow. Applause, applause. What do you think?"

Deb laughed. "Come on, Pat," she said punching her gently on the arm. "You know you love being up on stage.

What have we got to lose?" She smiled winningly at her friend. "Besides, the boys will get a kick out of it. Something for Bruno to write home to Paraguay about."

Pat smiled in spite of herself. "Okay, but why the heck am I the one who gets the tape left on her mouth? What's so funny about that?"

The other two just looked at each other, trying not to laugh.

"Tell the band we're in," Deb said. "And tell Phil if it gets a good laugh, he owes us one at Patsy's."

"Okay, so come five minutes before the show, and I'll tell you what to do. Thanks a lot! You're good sports. Oh, I've got to grab a bite. Will you bring this stuff with you when you come? Thanks again. Bye!" Jack went happily out the door.

Pat finished her salad and picked up the plastic dishes, looking around for a garbage can, and absentmindedly picked up the cuffs. "I've always wondered how these trick things work. Where was that release button again?"

Deb stood next to her and pointed. "It's sort of here, but they have to be engaged, I think, to have the button stick up."

Pat put one on her wrist. "Like this, you mean?"

"No," Deb replied, picking up the other set and trying one on her own wrist. "I think you have to lock both wrist manacles in order for it to work. Like this." She took the other cuff and locked that one, too. "See? Of course, it's not really funny unless you put the tape on your mouth so you can't yell at him when it doesn't work."

"What's so funny about that?" Pat asked, looking at the second wrist cuff and trying to find the button.

Deb smiled. "Pat, everyone knows how much you like to talk," she said. "Take my word; it'll be funny." She picked up the large roll of red tape with her two cuffed hands and

166

waved. "Here—let me show you," she teased.

Grabbing the roll away from Deb, Pat ripped off a piece with her teeth and stuck it on Deb's mouth.

"Hey," Deb mumbled through the tape, although it easily started to break away from her face. "That's not funny."

"Oh," said Pat, dancing back a little. "It seems funny to me." And she started to laugh. "Uh-oh, don't make me laugh. You know what happens when an old lady laughs too hard. Carl definitely did not say we could use the star's bathroom." She did her "If I hold my knees together, maybe I won't have to change my pants" dance.

Laughing now, too, Deb ripped part of the tape off and managed to put some on Pat's mouth. "There." She sat down and said smugly, "Now *that's* funny."

Pat pulled off the tape and sat down. The two women laughed like two hyenas, with their hands still in the cuffs.

Suddenly, they heard the big engine of the RV roar.

"What the ...?" said Pat, standing up just as the big bus went into gear. "What's going on?" She instantly realized that trying to stand up in a moving vehicle when her hands were handcuffed was no easy feat.

Deb frantically pulled at her cuffs, which instead of opening were tightening. "They won't come off!"

Pat lurched over to her friend, desperately holding on to the counter as the RV started to move down the hill.

"Who's driving this damn thing?" Pat spat out.

"Swearing, Pat?"

"You're damned right! Press this button, will you? I can't seem to reach it."

Deb reached out to press the spot. It might have worked if the RV hadn't just then hit a gigantic gopher hole and lurched sideways. They both fell in a heap the other way. It was a tangle of body parts and clothing as they hit the floor.

"Ouch!" Pat hit her head on a counter with a very sharp edge. "That's going to leave a bump. I'm beginning to not like this thing at all."

"Help!" yelled Deb, ripping off the rest of the tape that was stuck to her face. "Help! Stop!" Rolling over, she caught her cuffs on the chair leg as she tried to get loose. "Help, somebody!"

Pat struggled by pushing against Deb's backside. She managed to catch hold of the counter, despite the fact that the RV was now picking up speed as it crossed the bumpy field. "Mitchell is never going to believe this one," she groaned. "We'll never live this down."

"*If* we live," snapped Deb, still a prisoner to the chair leg. Her rear end was stuck up in the air. "Did it occur to you that it could be the killer who's driving this thing?"

"I don't care who it is," Pat answered, staggering toward the front panel attached to the cab. "I'm making him stop before he gets us out in the woods somewhere." Picking up Bruce Burnside's banjo case—and not caring if it was a collector's item—she banged on the wall with it. *Carl will not like this*, she thought grimly.

In the cab, Eric and Bruno looked questioningly at each other. "What in the world?" gasped Eric, who was at the wheel. "Did we hit something, or did something come loose in the back?"

Bruno shrugged his shoulders. "Not that I saw. We would have known if a deer had come out in front of us, right? You didn't hit a deer?" Bruno had become obsessed with the number of deer that people seemed to hit in Wisconsin on the roads.

Then it came again: *BANG, BANG, BANG!*

Eric swerved onto the little dirt road at the bottom of the hill, stopping just as he hit the one mailbox within five miles.

"Well, we definitely hit something now!" Bruno yelled. "Mi Dios, pensé que íbamos a morir!"

"Oh, snap!" Eric said, stepping hard on the brake. "If we wrecked the RV, Mom's going to take my driving privileges away for the rest of my life."

"And to think I thought about driving," Bruno mumbled, looking scared. "That would have sent me home to Paraguay."

Turning in the seat to his friend, Eric replied, "If you go, can I come, too?"

In the back, Pat fell down once again as they crashed against the mailbox.

Moments later, a voice could be heard outside, swearing quietly. "Who locked this flipping door?"

"Help!" yelled Deb.

Pat remained quiet—she'd recognized the voice. *Now, Lord, would be a good time. Take me now*, she silently prayed. The door was pulled open by a very surprised Detective LeSeur. Behind him were two scared boys.

"Gosh, it's Mom and Pat," Eric said, his voice shaking. "Mom, really, Phil just asked me to move it. It's not my fault."

"What in the world? Are you hurt? Who handcuffed you?" LeSeur asked.

Pat and Deb looked at each other. "It's really not our fault!" they said together.

Detective LeSeur had a lot of professional experience removing handcuffs. He helped the women out of the bus, freed them of their cuffs, and then wrote out a ticket for Eric. "And I don't want to see you driving until that license is in your hand," he said as he handed the ticket to the boy. As he turned to leave, they heard him mumbling, "I've got to find a different place to do a little volunteer work. Something easier, like maybe ... doing the Polar Plunge. Jumping into the big lake in January would be easier than this!"

Deb grimaced as she watched him walk off, laughing and shaking his head. *Sure, we weren't kidnapped,* she thought, *but someone did lock the door. I wonder who?*

Chapter Twenty-One

Pat's cell phone rang as she was driving to the church. "Didn't I turn that thing off?" she grumbled, trying to grab it from her bag. "Hello? Oh, damn!" she swore as she dropped the phone. Fumbling across the seat, she found it again and asked breathlessly, "Are you still there? Sorry; I dropped the damn thing."

"Tsk-tsk, swearing on the phone, pastor?" Peter said, and she could hear the smile in his voice. "I suppose it's because you were ... what? Locked in a mobile home? I've got to tell you, Agatha Christie couldn't have written it better." His deep belly laugh rang out loud and clear.

Pat pulled into the church lot, glancing to see which other cars were there. She did not want to have this conversation inside the church, where the staff might overhear it, not because she wanted hide it, but because they would probably laugh, too. *I get no respect,* she thought.

"Listen," she said teasingly, "I'm a married woman,

so you have to quit calling me like this. In addition to all the teasing I've endured this morning already, I feel like I've been in a train wreck. The good thing about a small town is that everyone knows your business and—"

"And the bad news is that everyone knows your business!" Peter said, jumping in.

"Besides," Pat grumbled, "how did you find out already?"

"Oh, I have my ways. We spies have spies."

"I'll just bet it was that darn LeSeur. Can't he mind his own business?"

"Actually, his question to me was, 'Can't those two biddies mind their own business?' It was a good laugh. Everyone here in the office enjoyed it immensely. We're thinking of putting it on YouTube." Then he sobered. "Seriously, Pat, I thought I'd warn you. Did someone lock that darn door, or could you have managed to lock it yourself by mistake?"

"No," Pat insisted. "Carl was there, but he left while we were still inside. I suppose anyone could have done it."

"Remember that, oh, wise lady. *Anyone* could have done it. And next time it won't be so funny."

Pat felt like a cloud had gone over the sun.

"I know it won't do any good," Peter continued, "but I'll say it anyway. Give this up. It won't be so funny on YouTube if you're dead." And with that, he hung up.

The sheriff's department in Washburn had been so busy with interviews and news reporters coming in that Suzie could hardly keep up with her online chat groups.

Give me the good old days, she lamented to herself, *when the biggest thing that happened was a speeding ticket or a cabin on the lake being vandalized.*

Tim and Barry, two members of the Canadian Fiddlers, came through the door. They looked scruffy, as if they hadn't slept all night. Neither of them spoke to Suzie; they simply stood by her desk, staring at her.

"Hey, Sally!" Suzie called out toward the back offices. "Looks like your ten o'clock interviews are here. Should I send them back one at a time or together?"

Sal's weary voice came from the back. "Send them both back. And can't you just please try to use the intercom?"

The two men smirked as they stood by the receptionist.

"Can't you?" she yelled back, nodding her head and indicating they could go back. Smiling to herself, she went back to her paperwork.

"Hello, gentlemen. Thank you for coming in. Please take a seat," Sal said, gesturing to the chairs in front of him.

"Is this going to take long?" Tim asked. "We did a gig last night, and now I just want to hit the sack."

So do I, Sal thought. *So do I.* He motioned toward two chairs in front of his desk. "Take a seat, and let's get started then."

After a brief interview, Sal excused the two guitarists. *I cannot believe I took this job,* Sal thought as he wearily put his feet up on his desk. He reached for the phone to call his wife to let her know he would be home late, but as he placed his hand on the receiver, the phone rang.

"Mayor on line one!" Suzie yelled from out front.

Why can't that woman use the intercom? he thought.

He didn't even have the phone to his ear before the mayor started in.

"What the heck is going on over there? Do you realize we've been getting calls from all over the country, asking us if it's safe to come up to Bayfield and the Tent! *Safe?* Our one and only office staff has gone home with a migraine. And the people at the Chamber of Commerce ... they can't get any work done because of the calls. When is this going to end? We hired you on LeSeur's recommendation, but you're still on probation. I want you in my office in the morning, to update the city council on the investigation. And you had better have made some progress. I'll bet those two sleuths from Ashland are probably doing a better job."

"Sir, we are doing the best we can," Sal replied, gulping down his anger. "If you want me to waste valuable time talking to those busybodies—no, strike that. I'm sorry. I'm tired and really quite busy. If you want to fire me, do so; otherwise, I'll see you tomorrow morning. Good-bye." He determinedly stopped himself from slamming down the receiver.

It rang again almost as soon as he'd hung up.

Surprisingly, the intercom buzzed. "Hi, boss. LeSeur is on line two. And just for the record, that mayor's been asking for it for a while."

Sal sighed and pressed line one.

"Hi, buddy," he heard as he picked up. "I know you're busy, but I just got some interesting information from a friend in the FBI that I think you need to know."

"I'm never going to get lunch," Sal groaned. "What is the point of having a beautiful wife if I never get to see her?" Looking up, he saw his heart's desire standing in the doorway, smiling. In her hands was a picnic basket. Suddenly, the day didn't seem so bad. "Listen, can I call you back in, say, a half an hour?" He looked up at his wife. "Or make that an hour, okay?"

"I guess this will wait. Call in an hour."

Sal hung up the phone.

"I just thought if you couldn't come home to me, I'd bring you a little something for nourishment," his wife said. Pushing aside the papers on his desk, she laid out a red checkered tablecloth and pulled out homemade soup and bread.

"You're wonderful," he exclaimed, kissing her soundly.

At the same time he couldn't help wondering what information was awaiting him from the FBI.

Deb and Pat headed off to work at the raffle ticket booth at the Tent once again.

"Two bucks, two bucks, two bucks!" Kay yelled as they came through the gate. "Hey, you two, you're late!"

Kay and Don are always early, Pat thought resentfully. *Don't they have a real life?* The couple's skill at selling tickets was legendary. Pat, overachiever that she was, was determined to outsell them this year. *Snap! Wouldn't you know she's already selling at the best spot?*

"I've already sold four books of tickets and five singles. Better hurry up, Pat, or I'll leave you in the dust!" Kay taunted.

Speed-walking to the ticket booth, Pat grabbed an apron and stuffed her pockets with pens, tickets, and the stickers that she put on buyers' shirts that read, "I've already bought raffle tickets."

"Cheesh, Pat, we're not twelve," Deb said, hurrying to catch her. "You don't actually have to sell more tickets than her, you know. She's, like, the queen of ticket-selling."

"Then I'm gonna be empress this year," Pat insisted.

"Immature!" Deb retorted.

Don laughed. "Fat chance you'll beat my wife tonight," he bragged. "She's already got her spot by the gate." Teasingly, he added, "Besides, aren't you just a little busy to sell tickets? I'll bet you'll be out there, grilling folks. You know, all 'tied up' in the investigation."

All the other ticket-sellers laughed.

"But I'm a pastor. I've been trained to talk people into

things," Pat said as she left the booth.

"Remember, Pat, we're just trying to raise money for upkeep on the tent. Don't harass people," Deb called after her.

"Yeah, yeah, like you don't count how many you sell. Raffle tickets, two bucks, two bucks, two bucks. Buy ten tonight, and get one free. Buy a hundred, and I'll buy you a beer." Hawking tickets, Pat headed for her favorite selling spot.

Don's remark was only the first that the two women would endure that night. By now, all the other volunteers knew about their adventure in the RV and were ribbing them mercilessly. The bruising didn't help. Luckily, Marc had bandaged them and tended to their bruises—after he'd stopped laughing. They were definitely teased that night, but they were too old to be too embarrassed.

With the bigger-than-usual crowd, and the women trying to sell lots of tickets, the time sped by. Pat didn't even stop to think about the time until she realized it was the end of the first set. The crowds came out of the tent, looking for a little snack and a beer. She stood outside the ticket booth and looked at her watch.

"Hurry up, Deb. They want us up there *now!*" Pat said impatiently, as her friend fussed with her sweater, which had somehow been buttoned wrong. Part of it was bunched up around her throat, making her look like a small child who hadn't quite figured out how to dress herself yet.

"Hang on," Deb replied, quickly rebuttoning. "Is this right?" she asked, looking at Pat for approval. "Boy, whose bright idea was it that we call out the winners every week?"

"I believe that would be you," Pat called over her shoulder. She hurried ahead of Deb toward the front opening of the tent, where the stage crew and stars entered. "Deb, did you bring the bucket with the tickets in it?"

"Oh, my gosh, I'd forget my head if ... be right back." Deb ran back for the bucket.

Pat sighed and went in through the stage entrance, her mind wandering as she waited to be called up on stage. *Suspects ... I just can't believe it's Linda or Forrest. That's the trouble. I never can quite believe nice people commit murder,* she thought, gnawing at the puzzle like a dog with a bone. *Of course, that's exactly who does it in the murder mysteries I read—the ex-lover, the quiet guy, the bad boy, or the estranged son. Murderers have no type. It's never the stranger from outside the village, no matter how much I wish it to be. I just can't figure out this murderer—or maybe the truth is that I just don't want to know.*

Leaning against the fencepost, she began mentally ticking off suspects while waiting for Deb. She could hear Ed on stage, making the audience laugh.

No, not Forrest or Linda, because they were both worried about each other. And it's just silly to think it's Sam. Girlfriends from the past, no matter how sordid the affair, only seem to add to interest in the Tent and in him, not distract from the band's popularity. This is the twenty-first century, after all. But this has become serious, and the longer it goes unsolved the more people will be hurt. Like Forrest. Of course, there is always the chance that the killer will get frightened or angry and do it again. She pulled her sweater closer around her chest, as if to shield herself from the thought.

Looking back through the tent flap, she saw Deb coming up hurriedly behind her.

"Ready for us?" Deb puffed.

"Just about." Noting her friend's heavy breathing, she gently chided, "Guess it's back on the treadmill for us, old girl."

"Oh, do shut up!" Deb responded. "And let's get this over with."

"I'd like to get this murder over with," Pat answered.

"Ready, girls?" Carl whispered from his spot by the stage stairs. "Be careful on the steps. This one's loose." He pointed to the first step with an old-fashioned gallant motion.

Deb hurried past him up the stairs, giving him a tentative smile. She was hoping that the big man had really forgiven them for questioning him about Linda.

Pat absentmindedly glanced down at the loose step and noticed something in the dirt. *What is that?* she wondered. It was something shiny, and for a moment, as she focused on it, she forgot the group waiting for her on stage. She leaned down to get a closer look, slipped on the gravel, and lost her balance. Her left foot went out, hitting the loose bottom step, and—*whoosh!*—down she went.

"Ooof! Darn, I thought those Wii sessions would have given me better balance." Focusing her eyes in the dark back stage, she looked at the object that had caused her fall. *Curiosity killed the cat,* she reminded herself, but she still reached out for the piece of metal buried in the dirt. She pulled it out of the dirt, brushed it off, and held it up in front of her to get a better look at it in the dim backstage light. *A tent stake?*

Then her eyes looked beyond the tent stake she held in her hand—and into the face of the killer. Her heart beat so fast, she thought she was having a heart attack.

Steady, old girl, she thought. *Oh, no. Not you. Please God, not him.* She knew—and it showed in her eyes. *Okay,* she thought, clutching her chest. *Maybe my heart will just break instead.*

He reached out as if to take the stake from her, and then, his face crumpling like one of last year's apples, he stepped back.

"Yes, I can see by your look that you've figured it out.

It was me," he said, tears welling up in his eyes. "But there's the start-up music, and like they say, the show must go on." Clearing his throat, he managed a small laugh. "Can we just finish this and talk afterward?" he pleaded.

"What's keeping you guys?" Deb whispered frantically from above them. "Anyone alive down there?"

Pat stared into his face, ignoring her friend. "Finish this?" She started to waver, but the guilt and remorse was written there for her to read, and there was no danger for her, as far as she could tell. "Okay," she said, taking a deep breath. And with their eyes, they made a pact to see it through to the ending.

"Let's go," he said.

And Pat followed Carl up onto the stage.

Deb stood smiling at the crowd, standing center stage as she waited for her friend to join her. *Where has Pat's sunshine personality gone all of a sudden?*

"What happened?" she whispered when Pat joined her. "Did you hurt yourself? You look like you've seen a ghost."

"No, my dear friend," Pat replied. She glanced over to Carl as she pulled a ticket. Raising her voice, she spoke loud and clear into the mike. "And this week's lucky winner is Nancy Hanson!"

Smiling and clapping with the crowd as the winner came up to receive her prize, Deb noticed Pat's eyes were not smiling.

Pat shook her head in response to Deb's concerned look. "No. No ghost but something much worse," she said as she wiped her eye.

Deb looked puzzled. "What's going on?"

"Later," Pat whispered, and she thought with regret, *I'll never think of this place in the same way ever again.*

Chapter Twenty-Two

That's the trouble with opening Pandora's Box, Pat thought. *Once you get a peek, you can't stop everything from rushing out.* She sighed.

Now that the show was over, the two best friends sat on green plastic chairs, with Carl's big frame dwarfing a chair between them.

"It was dark," he began, "just like tonight. It had been a crisp fall evening—one of those nights you could only have on the big lake. The northern lights made a show just for us. And it was like biting into a honey-crisp apple, or catching the damp earth smell of leaves under your feet when you walk along the shore in the early fog. The grounds were buzzing with activity. You know how it is. Of course you do. You two were even there. The last show had finished ... another successful season."

He drew on his pipe, and the sweet smell filled the air. "The cars pulled out of the parking lot, one by one, lights against the dark, making the trees stand out in relief—trees that lined the road back to real life; life outside the magical circle of the Big Top Chautauqua." He shook his head, as if in the wonder of it all. "Why that night? I've thought so many times since. Why that particular night? But I had to have it, you see. It was special ... part of the history, a part that made me connected to this place." He paused a moment, remembering.

"Some people, reluctant to leave the Tent and summer behind, lingered around the stage, where Mac and the band were pulling cords out of equipment, storing guitars carefully, and drinking beers from the case on the edge of the stage. I bought that case, you know, like so many before. They never even thanked me; never really invited me to share in their circle. Just as if they were gods and I ... I was nobody—the nobody they allowed to buy them beer. I could hear them, standing in the shadows, right about where we are sitting tonight.

"Well, you crazy Canucks," Mac said as he strolled across the stage trying not to show his impatience at their slow pace. "What we got here is a slew of stuff best put in the van by experts." Taking a drink from the bottle in his hand, he pointed it at Forrest. "Can you handle it on your own, do you think?"

Heinrich looked up and smirked. "In a bit of hurry are we?"'

Mac frowned. He never liked being teased about women, even obliquely, in front of his son. "None of that now. I'll just be finding my old guitar before I go. I won't be seeing you at the motel." And everyone knew he was off to meet his *latest amore.*

"And so it all began." Carl wiped his eyes as if he could wipe away the memory. "I slipped off into the barn, looking for my treasure—a keepsake of the season. I store a few of them you see, mementos of the place. I give my life to this place, these people," he said with a bit of fire in his voice. "I deserve it." Then sighing, that fire went out. "Anyway, there was an old poster, left by mistake when B.B. King was here. An early one that he and his band had signed. I ... I had to have it. And I had just found it out in that dark old barn and was tucking it into a folder under my arm, when he came in."

"Oh, and is it you, Carl?' Mac said, his voice heavy with disdain, like a king to one of his peons. "And what might you be doing out here all alone on Old Last Night? Can't be that your pilfering something, are you?"

"And then," Carl said, "he ... he *smiled*." Carl paused and looked up at the northern lights, all green and blue, changing each moment. Relighting his pipe, he continued, "I put up with all the jokes about my love of the Tent, always being left out of the inner circle. I understood they were all so special. But there I stood, with the evidence of my addiction in my hand, and Mac knowing about my trinkets. Even if he never told, he would *know.* I was enraged. I went toward him, and I guess I just pushed him. Pushed him away. Away from my little secret."

Deb put her hand out and touched his shoulder in sympathy, but she didn't speak.

"He fell forward, still laughing ... drunk ... knowing he had me in his pocket. And then ... he just lay there. I yelled at him to get up, to quit fooling around. 'You've had your fun,' I screamed at him. 'You crazy Canuck.'" Carl sighed heavily.

"But he didn't ... you see ... he didn't get up again."

The three of them sat without speaking in the quiet of the woods.

Finally, Pat broke the silence. "And so it all begins," she said, taking up his words and gently wrapping herself against the cold air in her husband's big coat. "Many big things begin with the little decision, the whim, the quick surge of anger." She sighed. "People always think small towns are sleepy little leave-your-door-unlocked, walk-safely-alone-in-the-dark kinds of places. Foolish, when you think about it." She looked directly into Carl's eyes. They sat for a moment feeling the peace of the place he loved most. "It's up to you, Carl. Choices, you see." She looked at him once more and stood up, putting her arm around Deb. They walked slowly to the car.

Carl waited, watching them leave. Looking around, he remembered all the laughter, the music, the good times. Then, wiping his eyes with his great white handkerchief and then blowing his nose, he put out his pipe, stood up, and walked over to where Sal was finishing up his volunteer job of picking up bottles and cans. Stopping at their car, glancing back, the two women saw Sal's face in the stage lights. First, a smile; then an incredulous look; and finally, Sal put his arm around Carl's shoulders. Slowly, the two men walked to his police car.

"It's good to live in a small town," Deb said. And for once, Pat had nothing at all to say.

Chapter Twenty-Three

It was a cold, misty, and gray June day. Deb stood on the front deck of the ferry boat, listening to the foghorn sounding in the forward distance. She and Pat had left Burton's Sunset Oasis Motel in Nova Scotia that morning, satchels in one hand and jackets in the other. Just two days earlier they had left Duluth en route to Minneapolis for their flight to Halifax.

"Isn't it gorgeous?" Deb sighed contentedly, turning to Pat. "Reminds me of the coast of Maine, only more mystical in all this fog.

"I'm so glad that Forrest and Linda invited us to meet them for the ceremony," Pat agreed. "I just can't get enough travel these days. And Cape Breton! What an exotic place! I never thought I would come here."

As they disembarked, Pat spotted Forrest standing on the dock in front of a green jeep, with what looked like a fiddle case at his feet. Forrest saw them and gave a hearty wave.

"Hey, Deb and Pat! Welcome! I am so glad you're here. It just wouldn't be right for us to go through this ceremony without you two. After all, you did so much to help my mother and me get through that terrible time. And if it weren't for you, we would never have known what happened to my dad." He smiled that boyish grin that so reminded them of his father.

"We really didn't do anything, Forrest," Deb insisted. "Nothing that anyone in our shoes wouldn't do. After all, who wouldn't be curious and try to figure out what happened in such strange circumstances?" She turned and gave him a big hug.

Forrest led them to the jeep and tossed in their bags and the fiddle. He beckoned them to squeeze in, then started up the engine.

They spent the day walking the beach and talking to locals.

Maybe Marc would like to come here with me sometime, Deb thought. *There's plenty of sailing.*

That evening, after Mac's ashes had been spread on the beach next to the Sunset Oasis Hotel, Deb and Pat sat on adjoining bar stools at the Fish Ball Tavern.

The mood was somber as Monty's remaining band members hooked up their mikes and tested their equipment, as though they were giving a professional performance at the Tent.

Consummate professionals at all times, Deb thought, marveling at the ability of people to go through the paces of their daily grind at times of sweet sorrow such as this one.

It had been comforting to see Monty's ashes sparkle in the midafternoon sunlight earlier that day. The beauty of the moment was tempered by the harsh reality of being confronted by their own mortality and the fleeting nature of life.

Returning her attention to the scene at hand, Deb was surprised to see Heinrich energetically setting up his drum set in the corner behind the mikes. Heinrich, Barry, and Tim had come along to the island at Linda's and Forrest's urging. *Probably guilted them into it*, Deb thought.

Heinrich had maintained the same level of abrupt grumpiness during the solemn memorial gathering on the beachfront that Deb and Pat had witnessed several weeks earlier at the Black Cat. He was the only one who had refused to take a turn at scattering the ashes.

"I wonder why he bothered coming?" Deb said to Pat.

"After all the years he played with Mac and despite his anger, there must still be some deep well of loyalty lurking in his soul," Pat replied softly.

"Where is Paul, the band manager?" Deb asked. "I haven't seen him today."

"Me either," Pat replied.

Linda went to the mike after the equipment was tuned and thanked everyone for coming. Then, surprisingly, with a wave to the boys in the band, she broke into a lovely ballad of "Love Lost." It was a sweet performance, filled with wistful nostalgia for what might have been. Deb looked over at Forrest, who had been gazing at his mother's face with a look of childlike wonder.

At that moment, the mood was broken by Deb's cell phone ringtone playing Pachelbel again.

"Turn that thing off!" Pat admonished, and Deb reached to do so. She glanced at the caller ID before she did. It was Eric calling, and there was no way she wouldn't take *his* call.

To her chagrin, Pat's phone vibrated. It was a text, so she opened her phone.

"Hey, it's Eric." Deb heard Eric's barely intelligible voice.

"Got some news for you. Can you guess what it is?"

"You didn't break up with your girlfriend on the eve of prom, did you?" Deb asked in mock alarm.

"No! What makes you think of such things? Much better. Dad took me in today, and I passed my test. I got my driver's license!"

"Oh, buddy, I'm so proud of you," Deb said quietly into the phone. "I can't wait to take that road trip out West in the RV that we've always talked about. Now we're one step closer!"

"I won't hit any more mailboxes; I promise," Eric replied happily.

"That's fantastic!" Deb cooed excitedly. "Now let me speak to Bruno, if he's there." Deb waited while the phone was passed to Bruno and then said, a bit too loudly in the crowded space, "Hi, Bruno! Hola, I mean!"

Deb's world was about to change in a big way. Bruno would be leaving the family soon to return home to Paraguay. A few short weeks after that, Deb and Marc would be taking in their two nephews, Eugene and Cliffy, who had been living in the foster home in New Jersey for the past four years. *Life changes*, she thought.

"So you want to know where you can get your flowers for your prom date?" Deb asked, winking at Pat. "Heike's, of course. She's the best. And tell her I said hello. And tell Dad that I said you and Eric can take the car out tonight! Goodbye, Bruno."

Sighing contentedly, her heart lightened by the call, Deb put away her phone and thought about the simplicity of young love. She marveled again at how lucky she was to experience it vicariously through her children to a small degree.

As Deb was talking to the boys, Pat was squinting as she tried to read her text. With a smile, she saw that it was from the official headquarters of army intelligence.

Hi P & D
Just to officially inform you, Peter asked me to send the following: Last night the FBI arrested four people, including Paul, the manager of Mac's band, for involvement in a smuggling operation. Not drugs but antiquities were involved. They cleverly put them in with all the band equipment. CIA was looking for drugs, so it took them a while to realize what was being brought in. Neither Mac nor any band members were involved. Andy Ross is disappointed that his first drug bust was a bust. I'm sure he would LOVE to hear from you two.

Rebecca Miller, assistant to Peter Thomas. His text address is pthomas@warnicke.com

I guess my son will have to teach me how to text after all, Pat thought with a smile.

Getting a nod from Forrest, Pat went to stand before the group. She looked around at all the musicians who had come to pay homage to a fellow traveler.

"Like Mac, I think we all feel—deep inside, past our cynicism—that there is something greater," she began. "Whatever we might call it, it's real to us all. So today, as we remember, we also put Mac into the hands of that something, trusting he will be cared for and loved. Would you join me in a prayer?

"Oh, Great Conductor of all that is, you make the very planets move in a rhythm of life and love. We thank you for this musician, this father, and this friend that you sent for a while to our particular part of the universe. Thank you for the wonderful songs he played. Today we gather to mourn his passing but also to celebrate his part in the great symphony of our lives. And to acknowledge that we will miss him in this love song we call life. We will remember him and his song with joy."

She smiled as she looked around. "And the entire universe sings *amen,* which means 'may it be so,'" she said to the group.

And a chorus rose up: "Amen!"

Then, Forrest stepped up to the mike and stood center stage before the gathered friends and family. He smiled at Linda, and his brown eyes danced. "This is for you, Dad," he said simply. Then he very smoothly reached behind him and pulled out Mac's fiddle, the same fiddle that he had spent his entire life avoiding. He placed the old fiddle under his chin and struck up his dad's favorite encore piece, "Farewell Friend."

*Yes, we've traveled the world together, up hill and down;
we've traveled the world together exploring sea and sound.
But now our paths are parting, you've other songs to sing;
And now my path goes on and beyond, under the goddess' wing.
So remember me to the children when you're telling our tale,
And remember me in the laughter, when you succeed and when you fail.
And remember me most my dear friends, in the music we both loved so.
Farewell for now, but don't be sad. It's only a word, you know.
Remember, remember, for I'll be waiting there for you.
Remember, remember, you've a place in her choir, too.*

Epilogue

It's good to be home, Deb thought as she stretched out on her deck chair and looked through the piles of mail that had arrived while she and Pat were away. She was enjoying the quiet. *This kind of quiet only comes when kids are in school and husbands, God bless them, are off working.*

Putting her feet up on the extra chair, she leafed through the envelopes, opening the ones of interest.

Hmm, electric bill, phone bill ... yikes, it's gotten bigger with all of us having cell phones. She shook her head. *Let's see ... city water bill ... a card from friends in Hawaii.*

Today, she didn't even feel the sin of envy that her friends owned a condo on Maui. *My life is pretty good ...* There was an announcement of coming movies at the film society from Ruth and Joel, a dentist bill, and a note from one of Bruno's coaches, telling them how much he enjoyed Bruno on the tennis team.

An auction flyer slipped out of the envelopes. She

nearly put it in the throwaway pile but then thought, *Maybe Pat will want to see this. She loves auctions.*

As she read it, she gasped loudly as she realized what it was. The heading read:

> ### Auction to be held at the Big Top of items from days gone by.
> Come bid on a poster signed by your favorite singer or drumsticks auto-graphed by musicians.
> List below.
> Once-in-a-lifetime sale.

She couldn't believe the amount of memorabilia that they were selling. There were two pages of items. *Could these* all *be from Carl's little collection? Wait 'til I show this to Pat,* she thought.

Deb picked up a simple green envelope next. Opening it, she clasped her hand to her mouth with glee as she read an invitation to a wedding reception for Linda and Sam. *I had no idea! Life is full of surprises!*

As she came to the bottom of the mail, an embossed envelope slipped from her hand to the deck. Picking it up, she noticed a faint scent. *Carolyn,* she thought. Opening it with her butter knife, she read:

Dearest Deb;
Although you have gone off the BigTop board, due to some recent changes your assistance is needed to help resolve a serious conflict in our organization.

As you may know, there is a movement among board members to erect a stat-ue at the foot of the ski hill to honor and memorialize all those who have made the Tent successful over the years. The challenge is that we can't agree who should be a part of the statue. I'm sure you can appreciate how so many peo-ple feel connected to and have a stake in this.

Even though we now know that a bronze statue is out of our price range, the idea is worthy enough that we would like to proceed by using your friend Pat's idea to have it carved by one of our local chainsaw artists out of wood.

We frankly need your mediation skill. Carl used to be so good at this. Please consider joining us for a committee meeting next Wednesday at 1 p.m. at Patsy's Bar.

Sincerely,
Carolyn

Deb put the date on her calendar, smiling at the mental image of a startled skier crashing into the wooden carving that Pat had suggested only as a joke. *At least there won't be a murder involved.* Then she knocked on her wood table ... just in case.

Recipes for When a Lot Is at Stake

TWICE POACHED WHITEFISH
(or Northern or Musky)
Linda's story and recipe from the church cookbook:

When I was a young girl growing up in northern Canada, my favorite place to go for lunch wasn't to the city with my mum, although that was fun, going on the train. No, my favorite was going to the lake. My dad and I would take our poles early on a sunny morning, with snacks and a thermos of hot tea, and while away the time, fishing. There we would be, sitting on the dock, reading the paper and arguing politics. By lunch, we would have torn apart many a politician and managed to catch a few fish, too. Off we'd head to Gilbert's, a place filled with men and great stories. The air was permeated with the smell of cooked fish.

Gilbert himself would greet us at the door, taking our fish and our newspaper, as we found a seat in the popular place. While we laughed and joked with Dad's friends, he would clean the fish, wrap it in our newsprint, and poach it. I can still see and smell it as if it were just yesterday. He would come back with it just a few minutes later, still wrapped in our newspapers, with plenty of chips and malt vinegar for each of us on the side. Gently, I would pull off the now-soggy paper, as if unwrapping a special present, and the skin would come off with it, leaving just the beautiful steaming white of the fish. It was so hot that I had to be careful not to burn my tongue, but so good, I didn't care if I burned it a little.

But what is the double-poached part, you may be asking, if you have read the recipe? Why, what every good Canadian knows. The fish was caught out of season, of course! *Poached!*

POACHING FISH

Whether fish is to be poached in a *court bouillon* or in plenty of salt water, or whether it is whole fish or simply a piece, it should be tied in a cheesecloth, leaving long ends free so that the fish can be lifted from the hot liquid without breaking.

The liquid must never boil but should always be kept at a simmer for perfect poaching.

A *court bouillon* is made with water, onions and carrots, herbs, wine or vinegar or lemon juice, and seasoning to taste. There must be enough liquid to completely cover the fish. Use two tablespoons wine, vinegar or lemon juice to half-cup of water (unless a recipe calls for other proportions). Lemon juice or vinegar is preferred with salmon; vinegar is used more often with shellfish.

Place all flavoring ingredients in the saucepan, add the liquids, and boil uncovered for twenty to thirty minutes before adding the fish.

If plain salted water is used for poaching, bring it to a full, rolling boil. When you are ready to put in the fish, remove the *court bouillon* or water from the heat. Once the fish has been added, bring the liquid to a simmer and continue to cook, covered, over low heat. Figure six to eight minutes per pound of fish, or allow ten minutes for every inch of thickness.

When the fish is done, remove it from the cooking liquid. To serve the fish cold, cool fish and liquid separately until both are tepid, and then pour enough of the liquid over the unwrapped fish to cover completely. Another method is to reduce cooking time and let the fish complete its cooking as the *court bouillon* cools. Refrigerate until cold. Unwrap and serve.

Poaching can also be done in the oven. Assemble the ingredients for the *court bouillon*; boil as above; strain. Then pour the liquid over the cheesecloth-wrapped fish in a baking pan. Cover the pan and place in preheated 375° F. oven. Poach for about ten minutes per pound or until the fish flakes easily when tested with a fork.

WHITE-WINE COURT BOUILLON

2 carrots, sliced

2 medium-sized onions, sliced

6 shallots, chopped

4 Tbsp. chopped parsley stems

1 tsp. minced fresh thyme

or ½ tsp. dried thyme

2 bay leaves

12 peppercorns, crushed in a mortar

1 Tbsp. salt

4 C. white wine

4 C. water

Other herbs or seasoning can be used. Also, the boiled *court bouillon* can be strained for top-of-the-stove poaching as well as for oven poaching.

WILD RICE SOUP

Pastor Pat's story and recipe for the church cookbook:

I know that every restaurant now serves wild rice soup, but the soup I remember comes with the memory of riceing.

When I was quite small, maybe five years old, I went riceing with my mother and her friends. I remember sitting in the strange boat that sat low in the water, going among the rice plants. The day was warm, and it could be that I was taken along simply because there was no one to watch me, but I didn't care. To me, it was an adventure!

The lake was called Rat Lake, and I spent some time looking for the creatures until I was assured by an auntie that there were none. The women were quiet, gliding among the plants, pulling them over the boat and knocking the heads with flat sticks. After a while, I fell asleep in the boat, lulled by the sun and the breeze and the swish of the rice.

I woke up at the dock pulled up to the house. I was suddenly really hungry, as only children seem to get.

"Can we have wild rice soup?" I asked.

The women laughed.

"Not today; this rice isn't ready yet," said Auntie. "But I'll make you some Sunday if you want." And she tousled my hair.

Forever after, I have loved wild rice soup and the memories of a riceing day!

WILD RICE SOUP

In a big pot, melt the butter over medium heat; add onion. Cook and stir about five minutes until goldeny beautiful. Add mushrooms and celery; cook and stir. Mix in flour, little by little. Gradually add broth, stirring all the while, until slightly thickened. Stir in cooked rice, and spices. Reduce heat to low. Stir in half & half and, of course, the sherry. Bring to simmer, stirring occasionally. And it's ready to eat! If you want to be fancy, after you put it in bowls, throw a little parsley or chives on top. You can also put in two precooked cubed chicken breasts, if you feel you have to, but the soup is great without them.

1/2 cup butter
/2 tsp. each: salt, curry powder,
1 lg. onion, chopped
paprika, dry mustard
2 1/2 cups sliced mushrooms
1/4 tsp. white pepper
1/2 cup sliced celery
2 cups half&half (don't use milk!)
1/2 cup flour
2/3 cup sherry
6 cups chicken broth
fresh chopped parsley or chives
2 cups cooked wild rice

MARC'S RATATOUILLE
A Chapple Avenue favorite
Story and recipe from church cookbook:

A great French stew for a hungry crew. And since it can be made without meat, a wonderful dish for those holidays when the college daughter comes home, announcing she is vegetarian.

I remember going to school, somewhere around third grade, and being offered—and then forced to eat—squash at hot lunch. Our teacher sat at the end of the table and gave everyone the eye and said, "Eat it and like it. It's good for you." Do you recall that yellow-orange leftover Elmer's glue-like stuff? All I recall is gagging it down and swearing off squash for life. That's it; I lumped all squash together as one inedible vegetable group. This was reinforced a few times later, as I was offered other nasty attempts at squashes, usually mashed, usually bland, and always overcooked mushy *blech*—a hard conception to overcome. Squash joined eggs and cheese as evils to be avoided.

Somewhere in my twenties, I was offered a zucchini and tomato dish that my mother had recently discovered, and it was not like anything I had had before. At first, I just ate the tomatoes, then wandered warily into what was left … and I liked it. It was crisp, flavorful, and actually delightful. The zucchini mostly carried the flavor of its neighbors, garlic, fresh basil, fresh tomatoes, onions. Simple, straightforward, inoffensive. Since then, I have been able to discover other joy in the squash family, though when it is done poorly, it still repulses me and sends me back to third grade, as I look for a corner under the table that needs caulking. I can't say that I have been as fortunate with eggs (still horrible) and cheese (please be kind and hide it well).

MY RATATOUILLE

A good-sized skillet, 10-12" helps. Cook on high heat.

Heat 2 Tbsp. olive oil in skillet until hot but not smoking.

Add 1 large onion sliced into large pieces. Fry 60 secs.

Add 2-3 sliced zucchini (round slices fairly even)

Stir quickly in, not over 60 secs more.

Add 2 medium very fresh tomatoes cut in wedges and 2-6 cloves diced or crushed fresh garlic

Cook another 60 secs until all heated through.

Black pepper to taste

Salt to taste

At the end, add a handful of fresh basil chopped (a must).

Add a splash of good balsamic vinegar (if you like)

or fresh Parmesan cheese chips (you will like this better than I do).

Let it rest a few minutes off the heat to meld flavors—in the pan if you like it softer, out of the pan if you prefer crispier.

Nice additions at times:

Fresh red sweet pepper, or a touch of hot banana pepper.

Fresh oregano

Walnuts

Yellow squash

One of my fondest childhood memories is of my mother baking fresh homemade white bread every Saturday. White bread was *the* thing in those days. A very early childhood memory was not of what doll I got for Christmas but of the wonderful, yeasty smell of rising dough.

When Marc and I first married, we lived in Ohio. In the fall of our first year there, an elderly woman in our community shared this recipe with us for beer-herb bread. I baked it for our Thanksgiving dinner that year, and we all loved it. It has been a staple of our Thanksgiving dinner ever since, as well as a standard comfort food for other times of the year. And of course, I'm always delighted when the kids get off the bus, running into the house, yelling, "I smell bread!"

From early fall to late spring, we observe "soup and bread" Sundays. Sunday evening dinner is always soup and bread, oftentimes, using this recipe.

We often use fresh herbs from our garden for this bread. It is fabulous slightly warm and with leftover turkey.

BEER-HERB BREAD

2 pkg dry yeast
1/2 C. lukewarm water
1/4 C. sugar
1 Tbsp. salt
1 12 oz. bottle/can of beer,
heated to lukewarm
2 Tbsp. melted butter/margarine
2 eggs, lightly beaten
1 tsp. sage
2 tsp. thyme
3 tsp. savory
1 small onion, grated
7 C. flour (approx.)

Sprinkle the yeast over the lukewarm water and stir to dissolve. Combine the heated beer, sugar, salt, and melted butter with the yeast mixture. Add the eggs, sage, thyme, savory, grated onion, and 4 cups of the flour, and beat until the mixture is smooth. Add enough remaining flour until the mixture becomes difficult to beat. Turn dough out onto a lightly floured board and begin kneading, adding enough of the remaining flour so that the dough does not stick to your hands or the board. Continue to knead until the dough is smooth and elastic. Place the dough in an oiled bowl, cover it with a damp cloth and let rise in a warm place until doubled in bulk, about 1-1/2 hours. When the dough has risen, punch it down, and let it rest for 10-15 minutes. Divide the dough in two pieces and shape each one into a round loaf. Place each in a loaf pan and let rise until double. Bake the loaves in a preheated 400° oven for 35 minutes. Remove the loaves from pans, and let cool on wire racks. This bread should be served slightly warm. You may also freeze the loaves and reheat as needed. This dough also makes wonderful dinner rolls or hamburger buns. Makes 2 loaves.

CHIPA GUAZU
(Paraguayan Corn Casserole)
Bruno's story and recipe from church cookbook

This recipe is from my mom in Paraguay. It is her family's version of a very traditional Paraguayan dish. It's delicious, sort of a cross between corn bread and a corn soufflé or pudding. You can eat it alone, like a casserole, or kind of like polenta, topped with or alongside a stew or chili.

My mom says, "I don't really have set measurements, but it's one of those can't-mess-up dishes. It always tastes good, even if it's not exact. It's great in the summer, when corn is cheap and abundant, but it's good in the fall/winter, too. This dish is always served at special holidays in Paraguay. This recipe will make a large Pyrex dish of chipa. You can halve it for a smaller batch.

CHIPA GUAZU

8 or more ears of corn (you can use frozen or canned if you must, but even out-of-season, fresh is better)

1 large sweet or yellow onion diced fine

1/3-1/2 cup corn oil

$^1/_2$-1 cup water

salt

6 eggs, separated

1-2 cups grated cheese (depending on how cheesy you want it)—any kind that melts well, like Colby jack or Muenster

1 cup milk, half&half or cream (depending on how rich you want it)

1 cup corn meal, regular flour, or a mix (corn meal makes it taste cornier, but flour works, too)

Cooking spray or a little more oil for the Pyrex

INSTRUCTIONS

1. Preheat the oven to 400°. Clean off the corn, and cut off kernels. Make sure to scrape the cob. If you want, blend all or $^3/_4$ of the kernels in a food processor or blender, for a creamier texture. If you prefer chunkier, leave the corn kernels whole. Put in a really big bowl; you'll mix everything into the corn.

2. Heat the oil in a deep frying pan on medium-low heat. Add onions before the oil is too hot. You do not want the onions to brown. You just want them translucent. Add enough water so the onions are submerged. Add 1 or 2 tsps. of salt, or as much as you think you'd like. You add it here so it dissolves and brings out the onion flavor. You may have to add more water as the onions cook down and the water evaporates. This is to keep the onions from browning. Cook the onions until they are very soft and practically invisible, about 10-15 minutes on very low heat. Take off the heat and let cool while

you do the next steps. There will be about 2-3 teaspoons of oil left with the onions, which will be added to the corn.

3. Beat the egg whites in a mixer until they make soft peaks. Then add the yolks and beat just until they are incorporated. Set aside.

4. Put the cheese, milk, onions, and oil in with the corn. Then add the cornmeal or flour and stir it well. Finally, fold in the eggs gently. If it's still really liquid, you may add more cornmeal or flour, but if it's oatmeal consistency, it's fine.

5. Spray the Pyrex with cooking spray or rub a little corn oil all over the bottom and sides of the pan. Pour in the mixture and bake for about 40 minutes to an hour, until the top and sides are brown and it's set in the middle (meaning it won't jiggle when you shake the pan). If you put in a toothpick, it will never come out completely clean. The chipa should be more like soufflé and less like cake or bread.

6. Eat it while it's hot and steamy, or cold as leftovers. Good for breakfast, lunch, or dinner.

RECIPE FOR FISH LIVERS

Here's the recipe, but if you just want to try them, several places in Bayfield have them on their menu. Seriously. My favorite is Gruenkes. Tell them Pat sent you. Don't knock 'em until you've tried 'em.

1 lb whitefish livers
2 Tbsp. flour
4 Tbsp. butter and 1 Tbsp. oil
Salt and pepper to taste

Dredge livers in seasoned flour and brown them in butter and oil but don't overcook. Serve hot.

A PREVIEW TO
NOW AND ZEN,
THE THIRD IN A SERIES OF
BEST FRIENDS MYSTERIES

The day the woman disappeared, Captain Mike got up early and took his two black labs out for a run.

Just like he always did.

He ate his oatmeal, grabbed his thermos of hot coffee, and kissed his wife absentmindedly.

Just like he always did.

Checking the sky for weather, he started to get into his old red Ford pickup.

Just like he always did.

On this day, he noticed a mature female eagle overhead and stopped for a moment to follow her flight as she soared, riding the winds off the big lake. Breathing in deeply the scent of water and sand, and still captivated by her, he watched in awe as she dipped to the water's edge, effortlessly picking up a large whitefish.

What might it be like, he thought enviously, *to fly with those great powerful wings on the currents like she does?*

Smiling, he started his old truck. Turning left, he headed to the lake and his Madeline ferry, parked at the Bayfield dock. He was eager to get the old girl out and fly, in his own way, on the waves of Lake Superior. Eighteen years as a ferry captain and his heart still beat a bit faster at the thought.

Just like he always did.

But this day wasn't like any other day. It was an ordinary day turned extraordinary by one single event. This was the day that what he "always did" changed forever.

ABOUT
BIG TOP CHAUTAUQUA:
A HISTORY

"Culture under the tent" enjoys a rich tradition in the Midwest. In 1874 the Chautauqua Assembly of Lake Chautauqua, New York, offered adult education in the sciences and the humanities. Soon after the turn of the century, traveling Chautauquas took the form of tent shows moving from town to town during the summer, offering lectures and entertainment. The town of Bayfield hosted several Chautauquas during the years preceding World War I.

Warren Nelson, a southern Minnesota farm boy, set the enterprise in motion with his vision to have a tent show at the base of the ski hill overlooking Lake Superior. Warren and his long-time partner, Betty Ferris, along with a few friends, moved to the area on a whim, set in motion by their love of the spectacular pristine beauty. They were attracted to a county with the proud distinction of having not a single stoplight located in its borders.

The origin of the current house show band started when Warren met Jack Gunderson, and later, other members of what was first called the Lost Nation String Band. That band evolved into what is now the Blue Canvas Orchestra: Bruce Burnside, the late great Don Pavel, Cal Aultman, Tom Mitchell, Bruce Bowers, and Severin Behnen. In recent years, Ed Willett and Andy Dee have joined up.

Some of the current members of the house show band have performed together for over thirty years. Because of that, their musical performances feel like the satisfying perfection of fine aged wine.

A permanent Chautauqua landed in Bayfield in the summer of 1986 after the talents of Warren Nelson and Betty Ferris and the Lost Nation String Band attracted the attention of community leaders in Bayfield, Ashland, and Washburn. The group had received rave reviews for their original musical histories produced and performed for three specific occasions: *Souvenir Views* for the Washburn centennial celebration; *Whistle Comin' In* for the Ashland centennial; and *Riding the Wind* for the Bayfield all-class reunion. Audience response to *Riding the Wind*—presented in the Bayfield High School gym—was so overwhelming that the group was asked to add an extra performance. Bayfield resident Mary Rice, along with the MAHADH Foundation (established by Mary Andersen Hulings and A.D. Hulings) offered to build a permanent theater that would showcase the myriad talents of these creative, experienced artists.

But Warren Nelson—a "man of the cloth"—had canvas in his blood after spending summers with his dad traveling to county fairs across southern Minnesota. He proposed a Chautauqua-style entertainment venue that would draw visitors from across the Upper Midwest to enjoy a variety of original productions, regional artists, and national headliners. The first tent and the first season topped Mt. Ashwabay

214

in the summer of 1986, offering 42 shows with 5,218 tickets sold. In 2009, 26,825 tickets were sold to 74 shows!

Funding provided critical financial support, but sweat equity was just as critical. When Lake Superior Big Top Chautauqua was incorporated as a non-profit corporation, officers Betty Ferris, Carolyn Sneed, and Tom Lindsey devoted countless hours to administering this new entity. Lake Superior Big Top Chautauqua had dozens of branch offices—the living rooms, dining rooms, cabins, and cars of everyone involved. Musicians, fans, and townspeople pitched in—literally—to set up the tent at the beginning of the season and to help keep things running smoothly throughout the summer.

A tradition of well-organized community support saved the life of Lake Superior Big Top Chautauqua in 2000 when the tent burned to the ground in the middle of the night as a result of an electrical short. Shrewd planning and some good luck had provided a back-up tent. The season lost only one night of performances.

Lake Superior Big Top Chautauqua continues to advance its own mission and stay true to the ideals of the original Chautauqua movement by touring during the off-season, to schools and community theaters throughout the region. Tent Show Radio is beamed into the homes of families on 53 public radio stations across the country. The Lost Nation String Band is still together and their music is heard on CDs, videotapes, DVDs and mp3 files—media that didn't exist when they first started performing together. Digital images have replaced thousands of slides used to illustrate songs and stories of the past in our Chautauqua Original Musicals.

At the start of a new decade, the magic of Lake Superior Big Top Chautauqua nestles comfortably next to its competitive cousins—radio, television, and the Internet—to

215

tell stories of those who walked the land and paddled the rivers and stared at the stars and dreamed of what the next day would bring.

A lot of strong individuals like Betty Ferris, Carolyn Sneed, Carol and Jerry Carlson, Phillip Anich, Therene Gazdik, Sally Kessler, Liz Woodworth, and Cheryl Leah, also contributed great talent and gritty determination over the years to build the organization into what it is today. Betty Ferris collaborated with Warren on the historical research and writing and has been the archivist and the photo technician for twenty-five years. Carolyn Sneed, the long-time executive director, oversaw the nuts and bolts of the organization for many years. Carol and Jerry Carlson, the real life caretakers of the ski hill and occupants of the A-frame, have overseen food service on the grounds since the beginning. Phillip Anich, the operating manager and performer and Sally Kessler, Liz Woodworth, and Cheryl Leah are some of the wonderful creative talents who still perform regularly at the tent.

The summer of 2010 marks the twenty-fifth season of facilitating the production and presentation of quality, affordably priced entertainment, suitable for the entire family. Through the commissioning of new productions, focusing on themes of regional historical and cultural significance, Lake Superior Big Top Chautauqua serves as a base of support, offering artistic employment opportunities to local and regional artists and technicians.

FOR MORE INFORMATION OR TO ORDER TICKETS TO A SHOW GO TO:
www.bigtop.org or call 888-BIG-TENT or 715-373-5552

ABOUT THE AUTHORS

Co-authors Deb Lewis and Pat Ondarko really are best friends who live in Ashland, Wisconsin, on the south shore of Lake Superior. They have previously penned *Bad to the Last Drop*, a mystery novel set in Ashland. When not escaping into the adventure of mystery novel-writing, Deb is a practicing family law attorney, and Pat is a Lutheran minister. *Too Much at Stake* is the second in the series of Best Friends Mysteries. They are working on their next mystery novel, *Now and Zen*.